THE X HOUNDS

Thick Brick

Copyright © 2024 Thick Brick
All rights reserved
First Edition

NEWMAN SPRINGS PUBLISHING
320 Broad Street
Red Bank, NJ 07701

First originally published by Newman Springs Publishing 2024

ISBN 979-8-89308-568-6 (Paperback)
ISBN 979-8-89308-569-3 (Digital)

Printed in the United States of America

To my parents, former and current teachers, family, friends, my churches, my preachers, professional wrestling, my people from the countryside, those who support me, God, my football coaches, my teammates, creative thinking, to whom and what inspired me, and to the greatest characters in this book.
Salute!

CHAPTER 1

Tragedy

"June 14th, 2069," Professor Moshk said as he spoke into his voice recorder.

"Finally, I've calculated all of my intel. Maybe the world won't think I'm such a screwup for once. I'm not asking for fame, just to be a noticeable hero. With a few more tests, my research will not only be complete but also world-changing. I call this technology Project 1B86-0D, aka the Anti-Illness X-Venom Process: the Method to End All Sickness. Illnesses include all flu types, cancers, and every other sickness out there. I simply asked myself: 'What do these illnesses have in them? What can possibly fight the bacteria in it?'

"And then it hit me. I simply searched and searched and searched, only to find no answer. I dedicated my entire life to this. All I want is world peace to be present and world chaos to be nothing but a hilarious myth. If my calculations are accurate, and boy, do I hope they are, I should have a completion rate of 93.02%. This operation requires three highly advanced knowledge officials to complete. And thankfully, Dr. Meetho, Grande Andre, and myself are those three brave individuals who share zero ignorance in science, math, and even technology."

Thick Brick

"Uh, Professor. Do you maybe wanna shut up and get over here to help?" Dr. Meetho said in a sarcastic voice.

"Give me a minute," Professor Moshk responded. "I'm documenting our research into my voice recorder, just in case."

"Well, maybe my fist should document its markings in your face. Research that," Dr. Meetho said.

"Okay, I know you're not threatening me," Professor Moshk responded.

"Hey, guys, come on now!" said Grande Andre. "Now we're all great friends. There's no good reason to fight here. So let's all just relax, eat some food, drink something, and get this done. Agreed?"

"Agreed," Professor Moshk said.

"Yeah, no problem," said Dr. Meetho.

"Sorry, Doc," Professor Moshk responded. "It's just, I know how important this is to you and Andre, so I just want it to be successful."

"I know," said Dr. Meetho. "We should all just sit down, eat, drink, and just talk."

"Well said," said Grande Andre. The three men sat down and did just that. Once they finished, they put on their lab coats, shiny black gloves, sunlight-resistant goggles, and their deodorant and got to work. The lab they worked in was in space and later became known as the Top-Secret Examination Lab (or TSEL for short). "Hey, Dr. Meetho," Andre said.

"Yes, Andre?" Dr. Meetho responded.

"How is this supposed to work again?" Andre asked.

"Once you take the baking soda and pour it into the gallon, you simply wait until it reaches up to thirty-six ounces exactly in order to drop a tiny bit of dissected mouse guts into it. And remember, once you see an orange sunlight glow, that means it's working. Now this will very likely occur twenty-four seconds after you've done so. And one last thing, whatever you do, do not, DO NOT, take your goggles off! I promise you, your eyesight will forever decline," said Dr. Meetho.

All three men did what they were supposed to do, and everything went as predicted. Out of the blue, a random beeping noise appeared on their radar.

The X Hounds

"Hey, Andre," Professor Moshk said.

"Yeah, Professor," he responded.

"Do you mind checking out the radar to see what's up?" asked Professor Moshk.

"Yeah, I'll go ahead and see what's up," Grande Andre said. When he went over to see what was up, he thought the radar was just a little bit messed up because it needed to be fixed anyway. So he ignored it and said to the others, "It's nothing bad. It needs to be fixed though... *Doctor*."

"I told you, I'll fix it myself...eventually," Dr. Meetho said.

"Or," Andre began, "you could just press ten little buttons on a phone and call the insurance company!"

"You dumb, lipidic zygote!" Dr. Meetho responded. "Do you know how much money the insurance company is going to try to pull out of our rectums for just a little glitch in the computer system?"

"Look here, Anus Woblet," Andre said. "I told you, stop calling me names, or I'm quitting!"

"Okay, sorry," Dr. Meetho responded. "Sorry, I'm just hyper 'cause I really feel like, for once in my life, I'm not going to fail."

"It's fine," Andre said. "We all just need to forgive and move on. It's the only way for us to stick together, progress, and get stronger."

"You're right," Dr. Meetho said. "Now let's get back to the project." Once they saw a sunlight-orange glow, they all got excited. "Yes! My research has worked! Woo-hoo!"

Or at least, he thought. They heard a beeping noise for the second time, and this time it said what was happening. It said, in a robotic voice, "A giant asteroid field near you has caught fire due to the close proximity of chemicals. One asteroid is heading your way and could cause a major tragedy in T-minus seventeen seconds. I recommend heading for the nearest escape pod if you would like to have the ability to finish your research. In other words, get out or die."

"Get to the escape pod now!" Dr. Meetho said in panic.

Once they got in, Professor Moshk asked him, "Doc, what about your research?"

"None of that matters anymore!" Dr. Meetho responded. "We need to go before we blow!"

Thick Brick

They tried to escape, but the pod could not release fast enough. Not only that but the computer was also off by a terrible eight seconds. Before it could release in time, the burning asteroid hit the TSEL headquarters in space. It exploded greatly and became nothing but space debris.

All of their research, destroyed. And as for Professor Moshk, Grande Andre, and Dr. Meetho, they were no more because they died. Make no mistake, what happened here today was, indeed, a tragedy.

CHAPTER 2

The Rise of Terror

On the planet known as Amure-X, the only planet with human life, three men (known as the Uncharted Titans Huskin, Bronco, and Seth) were a tag-team trio in a professional wrestling industry known as CXW, which was short for Crazy Xtreme Wrestling.

One night, they were wrestling three men known as Germ, Wreck, and Rude. Rude got his nickname because he was the biggest…jerk, to put it nicely. Anytime women would be around, he'd try his best to leave with them. He got smacked in the face every time but somehow never learned. Wreck received his nickname because all he had to do was lose his balance and something would break. If it was cake, it would lose its batter. If it was glass, it would shatter. Basically, he's clumsy. Germ obtained his nickname because he was always dirty. His language, his hands, everything about him.

The match was a tables elimination match to crown the first-ever CXW World Champion, CXW Amure-Xian Champion, and the CXW Annual Champion. The rules of this match were to put your opponent through a table, and that opponent would no longer be in the match, forcing them to return to the locker room. "The fol-

Thick Brick

lowing contest is a tables elimination match for the CXW Annual, Amure-Xian, and World Heavyweight Championship!" yelled the ring announcer.

When the bell rang, all six men were going at it for some time until eventually, Seth rolled under the bottom rope and pulled a table out from under the ring. But Rude stopped him from putting the table in the ring. They began duking it out at ringside until Rude grabbed Seth by the arm and threw him into the ring post face-first. This allowed Rude to collect the upper hand, so he hesitated not. He then set the table up, and shortly after, he attempted to get a hold of Seth. But Seth soon retaliated. He jumped onto the apron, ran to Rude, jumped off, and kicked Rude dead center in his nose. Rude fell hard.

He had a few tiny droplets of blood which was caused by the force of the kick. Seth took the time to grab a rope out from under the ring, and he would use it to tie Rude to the table. Seth made sure the pressure would remain on Rude so Rude would never stand a chance. To make certain of this, Seth grabbed another item. And that was a weapon. The weapon he would utilize would be a steel chair with barbwire wrapped around it. Intense, right?

Anyway, Seth utilized this weapon with "chairlessness." Huh, see what I did there? A careless Seth was determined to win. Not just for himself, not just for his teammates but to also become a man women drooled over. And in the end, that's what it all boils down to for all three. He delivered chair shots to the back, the stomach, and also the face.

As an obvious action, Rude would yell out in extreme pain. And the best part (also the part that matters most), the crowd adored it. They couldn't stand Rude, Wreck, and Germ. In wrestling terms, they would be classified as heels or bad guys, whereas Huskin, Seth, and Bronco were good guys or baby faces.

Once Seth felt the need to stop hitting Rude, he dragged him over to the table and laid him on top of it. Seth gave another chair shot just to be safe. Seth then sat Rude up so he could put the chair under Rude's back. Once Seth did this, he slammed Rude down on the table, causing Rude's back to lay on top of the chair. To make sure Rude couldn't get away, Seth tied him to the table using the rope.

Once Rude was tied in a knot, the only thing left to do for Seth was to eliminate Rude. Therefore, Seth got on the top rope, jumped off, performed a very well-executed reverse backflip, and landed on Rude. This made the table break, which meant Rude was eliminated from the match. I guess it's safe to say Rude was "knot" going to win that match.

Bronco and Huskin were still duking it out with their opponents. So Seth decided to go and help Bronco, given the fact he was fighting the strongest one, which would've been Wreck. Meanwhile, Huskin was having a bit of a hard time trying to take out Germ. Anytime he attempted a move, Germ would counter.

Germ had Huskin by a long way. When Germ was just about to strike Huskin with a long wooden stick, he decided to taunt Huskin first. Germ put his hand under the chin of Huskin and said, "You think you're so powerful, huh? Prove it!" He then finished his statement with a slap across the face of Huskin.

And for Huskin, that was all it took. He stood down on one knee, and Germ grabbed the wooden stick. He then raised as high into the air as he could and, full force, swung the stick at Huskin. However, the stick was caught by Huskin. At this moment, Germ knew he messed up.

Huskin ripped the stick out of the hands of Germ and began to strike him with the stick. Huskin snapped. He knew nothing would stop him from possibly injuring Germ. Germ deserved it, though. He bullied everyone in all of CXW. Huskin never wanted to intentionally hurt anyone until he met Germ. Huskin was a chill dude and didn't care what people thought of him because he was happy with himself. But he could not stand the idiocy and stupidity at all.

Huskin had a look of anger in his eyes. Livid, angry words could not describe. He would have vengeance for everything Germ ever did to other people and to Huskin. Huskin would no doubt stand up for himself, but he hated bullies going after people who couldn't.

Huskin rolled Germ into the ring only to continue this heinous assault. Huskin hit him a few more times with the stick until he

Thick Brick

got an idea. He remembered the lighter in his pocket and lit up the wooden stick. Huskin knew the wood would burn quick, so he gave as many shots as he could. He repeatedly struck Germ with the flaming wooden stick for about seventeen seconds until the stick broke across Germ's back. Huskin, from the force of his power, left burn marks on Germ's back. Then he went to ringside to grab a table from under the ring, but Germ saw him. Germ got on the top rope and jumped off going after Huskin, but Huskin caught him. He caught Germ and held him on his shoulders. When Huskin was ready, he flipped Germ onto his back, making him land on top of the barrier.

Germ already felt great pain, but he couldn't balance on top of the barrier. He rolled over and landed on the floor. He couldn't move; he was outnumbered anyway. Huskin set the table up against the barrier on a slant so he could run into his opponent, making them break through the table for elimination but also go through the barrier to inflict more pain. He wanted Germ to hurt badly. He even wanted Germ's entire wrestling career over. So he put Germ on his right shoulder and ran around the ring a few times.

Once Huskin finished his laps around the ring, he threw Germ into the table so hard he ended up going through the barrier. This made the second elimination, leaving one more opponent to be beaten by three men. When Huskin looked over at Bronco and Seth, they were practically mugging Wreck. But what Wreck didn't know was, he was about to get wrecked bad. Huskin walked over to them and said, "Boys, we need to end this quick. I'm starving, I'm thirsty, and I'm in the mood for some milkshakes."

"It honestly doesn't surprise me that you're hungry," Bronco said. "But I will admit, I feel the same way."

"Yeah, boys," Seth said. "Let's get this dude through a table. I was thinking about the good old KLF. The Kick Launch Flip."

"Agreed," Huskin responded. Huskin cleared off the commentary table and stood on top of it. Bronco pulled a twenty-foot ladder out from under the ring and put it in the ring. When Huskin saw the ladder, he decided to get his own twenty-foot ladder. He set up the ladder in front of the commentary table and climbed to the top of it. Seth dragged Wreck over to the entrance ramp and left him there, lying. He

The X Hounds

then went back to the ring to grab the steel chair wrapped in barbed wire and even a grappling hook. He set the steel chair under the face of a face-down Wreck in order to get set up for his next move.

Wreck managed to get on his hands and knees, which then allowed Seth to run up to him, put his foot on the back of Wreck's head, and stomp his face into the barbed wire wrapped around the steel chair. This allowed Seth to get enough time to throw the grappling hook to the bars near the roof of the arena. Once he got a perfect grip, he then climbed to the top of the titantron and waited for Wreck to stand up. Once Wreck stood up, Seth came swinging from the top of the titantron and, full force, kicked Wreck in the middle of his stomach.

Wreck went flying through the air. He went so far and high that Bronco did a handstand on top of the ladder, locked Wreck's head in between his ankles, used his legs as a launcher, and launched Wreck on top of the commentary table. Wreck was defenseless, and Huskin knew it. Huskin jumped off the top of the ladder, performed a spinning backflip, and landed on Wreck, smashing him through the table. "Kick launch flip! The kick launch flip!" One of the commentators yelled. "And Seth, Bronco, and Huskin are your new champions!" This became the third elimination on the team of Germ, Wreck, and Rude, and the final elimination of the match.

The entire crowd erupted and screamed out of joy. People were crying tears of joy, yelling, and running around like imprudent idiots. Then the ring announcer came to the ring and the three men awaited to be crowned champions. When he got in the ring with the three men, he held all three titles and crowned all three men with their titles. He then said, "Here are your winners, and new CXW Annual Champion, Bronco! And your new CXW World Champion Huskin! And finally, your new CXW Amure-Xian Champion, Seth!" The entire crowd still yelled, as they couldn't believe they essentially won. Bronco then got the microphone from the ring announcer and gave a small victory speech.

"Wow," he said. "It's just so unbelievable that this actually happened. I am just so happy to hold this title for at least a year, and what I really mean is us! We are the ones who fought to wear

Thick Brick

THIS TITLE! YOU GUYS ARE THE ONES WHO HELPED ME DEFEAT MY GIANTS! YOUR LOVE! YOUR SUPPORT! If I could wrap this entire title around the entire fanbase of CXW, I would. Because YOU are the real champions here! And let me tell you, if anyone tries to take this title away from me next year, or anytime, they will suffer! I will defend this title the way it's supposed to be defended. Once a year. And until I retire, I am your CXW annual champion." The crowd gave a deafening round of applause and support for Bronco. Bronco then handed the mic to Seth, and Seth gave a speech.

"Thank you all," Seth said. "First off, I would like to thank my best friends, Bronco and Huskin, for all of their support and fighting by my side this whole time I've been in this business. But I also want to thank my other friends. And that's you! It's YOU! THE ENTIRE CXW UNIVERSE! THANK YOU! I am your first ever CXW Amure-Xian Champion, and I promise you, it's not gonna be any other soul, ever! And let me tell you, I will annihilate any arrogant zygote who tries to take it from me! Try me! I dare you with all two hundred six bones in my body! Test me! Try to pass my test! I promise you! You will make a zero." The crowd applauded him as he handed the mic over to Huskin so he could make his speech.

"Thank you all," Huskin said. "It's all because of you that I am top dog in this company. That and because of my brothers. These guys have always treated me with the utmost respect. We all support each other and provide the utmost respect. We are the top three in this business, and you can write all the inequalities you want. But at the end of the day, no one is better than the Uncharted Titans!

"The Uncharted Titans will not only stand up against thieves but will find a thief's end and chase a fortune of a lost legacy. And that is a BROTHERHOOD! And the reason why I have been named top dog in this company is because not only am I the CXW world heavyweight champion. I am the most dangerous man in all of professional wrestling!" He then threw the mic down on the mat and walked backstage with Bronco and Seth.

Once they were backstage, they all high-fived and celebrated the biggest victory of their career. "All right, boys," Seth began. "Where are we going for dinner?"

The X Hounds

"I know just the place," Bronco said. They all rode in Huskin's truck to Rexton Bar and arcade. Once they arrived, they ate pizza and breadsticks and drank soda. And for dessert, they all had chocolate milkshakes with tiny chocolate bars crushed up inside. Once they finished their dinner, they gamed away in the arcade for hours. Once they were ready, they decided to take a nice long joyride through the city of Rexton. While they were riding around, something a hundred percent unexpected occurred. An enormous rock with blazing green flames shot across the sky. When it hit the ground, it resulted in a loud bang.

"Uh, does anyone else feel like a little detour?" Huskin asked.

"Yeah," Bronco responded.

"Let's go check it out," Seth suggested. They drove over to check out what was going on. When they arrived at the site of the wreckage, they got out and stood in front of the asteroid. They didn't even know what to say or do. They just stood there, wondering. After some time, they decided to touch it. It was smoother than the top of a jellyfish. When they grabbed a piece from the asteroid, they held it in their hand for a short amount of time. They noticed it formed into a ball, but what would happen next was illogical.

The ball enlarged, and they were surprised. They never saw anything like it. And nothing could stop what happened next. Each ball exploded acid all over them. They received horrible burns. Skin was melted. Bones were visible. There was a loud yell from all of them because the pain was too much. They fell on the ground and didn't do a thing after. They couldn't move from the pain, so they stayed there.

Then the asteroid began rolling toward them. They knew, either way, they were going to die. *So why bother?* is what they thought. Finally, the asteroid was on top of them, and they couldn't breathe. Soon their eyes would shut, and they would stop moving.

Once they stopped moving, the asteroid became smaller. It was shrinking into their exposed flesh and bones. When it stopped, a green and black glow shined all over them. They became...inhuman. Hair appeared all over their bodies, their teeth became bloodred and chainsaw sharp, and muscles were tripled. They—all three—opened

Thick Brick

one eye, and no eye color or pupil was there—only a burning flame. They became precisely what they despised: evil, feared, bullies. Except, they were worse. The reason for this was the explosion and or tragedy which destroyed TSEL. This came from the substances and mixed chemicals which formed in the asteroid.

But what contributed to 85.76% of this mutation was the Anti-illness X-venom vaccine. All they knew how to do was hurt. They became nothing but the most feared beasts in all of Amure-X. All they wanted was to tear the innocent people apart—literally. All they would do at night was run all over the walls, jump from building to building, chase away the good, and even steal food from local mom-and-pop stores and restaurants. If this happened to me, I'd at least have the decency to rob corporate. Anyway, one woman tried to run them over with her semi one night. But it didn't end well for her. Bronco ran directly in the middle of her truck, and she put full force on the gas pedal.

"You betta move out the way! Or I'll gladlae hit cha!" she said. Well, turns out she did hit him. But not the way she imagined. When the truck got close, Bronco slammed his head into the front of the truck, causing it to flip over him high into the air. When she came crashing down, the truck exploded. Thankfully, there was a fire department nearby to put the fire out. The woman escaped the fire thanks to the airbag. When the fire department arrived, the fire was put out, but the woman suffered a broken femur and a damaged kidney. It was unknown if she would survive or not. This angered the hounds. Therefore, they barked and howled on an endless track, running around to wreak havoc elsewhere—or so they thought.

"BNY 22 notifying, I have a visual on one member of the unknown species. I'm ready to shoot," she said.

"BNY 22, this is EML 6," she responded. "I've located a second, and I'm prepared as well."

"This is LCY 19 giving permission to fire. I'm formulated for a shot. Fire at precise aim," she said. When these three girls fired, the hounds were shot in cold blood in the neck with a dart which made them fall into a lengthy deep sleep.

CHAPTER 3

The CTA

When the hounds were shot, they were asleep for about two hours and seventeen minutes. When they awoke, they discovered they were trapped inside a chamber pod. They had no idea what happened. They viewed the site which stood in front of them, and that was a site of three beautiful women. "Who and what mutation are you?" EML 6 asked.

"I'm Huskin," he said.

"I'm Bronco," he said.

"And I'm Seth," he said.

"I don't care," EML 6 said.

"Then why did you even ask?" Seth asked.

"Because I'm aggressive!" EML 6 responded.

"I am so in love with her at the moment," Huskin said.

"Don't try to sweet talk us!" BNY 22 said.

"We couldn't be any sweeter than you," Bronco said.

"Shut up!" BNY 22 yelled as her cheeks became red.

"Why are you so determined to terrorize the entire planet of Amure-X?" LCY 19 asked.

"Terrorize?" Seth said in confusion. "What do you mean terrorize? We want to protect Amure-X!"

Thick Brick

"Roll film," LCY 19 said. The three men couldn't remember anything. They watched the video of what happened to them and what they have done, and they felt great shame.

"I don't even know what to say right now," Huskin said.

"How does something so…bizarre even happen?" Seth asked.

"I-I don't even, know," Bronco said as a tear fell down the side of his face. "What is even happening? Can you please, at least, elaborate on…this?"

"We took the time to look back at the last two days of your lives, and we saw what you really are," EML 6 said.

"Yeah," Huskin began, "treacherous, evil, demons."

"No," EML 6 began, "protective, caring, and dominant."

"Care to give us your names?" Bronco asked.

"Sure," LCY 19 said. "I'm Lucy."

"I'm Brittany," BNY 22 said.

"And I'm Emily," EML 6 said. Huskin looked at her with a look he never had before. He was in love. What he loved most about Emily was, she was just like him.

"Now look," Brittany began, "we have to bring you to the Wise-Minded Critical Thinker, Baron Gunn. But we all just call him Baron. We also have to bring you to him chained up because of what your mutations have done."

"It's fine," Seth said. "We understand."

"Good," Emily said. "Come with us." The three men were released from their chambers and chained up to take them to Baron. When they arrived at the doors of the Wise-Minded Critical-Thinker, Emily gave a knock and waited for the door to open.

"So," Huskin began, "who exactly is this…thinker dude?"

"He's been ranked the fourth smartest, unique being in all of this universe," Emily responded. "I say being because of his education."

"What's his education?" Huskin asked.

"That's the thing, we don't know." Said Lucy.

"All that's been confirmed is, he's inhuman," Emily said. "Not only is he inhuman but he's also my brother."

"Come forth unto my throne," Baron said. They opened the doors and saw Baron sitting in his chair on top of his throne of twelve

The X Hounds

steps, and the back of his chair was facing them. "What are their names Emily?" he asked.

"Huskin, Bronco, and Seth," she responded.

"And their last names?" Baron asked.

"We…don't know," Huskin said. "We're just great friends who were born with natural talent for wrestling. We're also the top three in CXW."

Baron turned his chair around with one of the buttons on the ledge and said, "Interesting." He took a long stare at the hounds and tried to figure out what caused the asteroid to do this. "I can't figure out what happened, but I can try with time," Baron said. "But I know what I can do. Those darts aren't going to be enough. They only last three hours. You have only thirty-eight minutes, so be quick. I need you to take a ship back to Amure-X and go to Rexton Bar and Arcade to find a man by the name of Jaykon. This man is nothing but a criminal. He's committed every crime there is but somehow manages to escape imprisonment. I will supply you with duct tape, a strap, and flour. Use the strap to hit him until he's defenseless. Use the duct tape to tie him up so he can't run. And use the flour to throw in his eyes so he can't see. Do the job and get back here. Take a ship from the garage and bring Jaykon back. You should catch him with a bottle of Messy Rex Shine and a pizza. He should be wearing a red jacket with a light blue J on the back. Now I'm trusting you. Which is why I'm removing the chains. And one other thing, what does CXW mean?"

"Crazy Xtreme Wrestling," Seth said. "We'll get the guy. Don't worry about that."

"Thanks," Baron replied.

"What does CTA stand for?" Bronco asked.

"Critical Thinker's Agency," Baron answered.

"All right, let's go," Huskin said. They jumped on the ship and headed for Rexton Bar and Arcade and hoped to find this man before their time expired.

CHAPTER 4

Hunting Jaykon

They began to travel to Rexton Bar and Arcade in hopes that they could catch this guy. Once they arrived at Amure-X, they landed their ship in a field behind the bar and turned invisible mode on. "All right, boys," Bronco began, "remember to look for a guy with a red jacket with a blue J on the back."

"Be vigilant for a bottle of Messy Rex Shine in his hand too," Huskin said. They walked through the front door and saw Jaykon sitting in the booth eating Alfredo-sauce pizza and drinking Messy Rex moonshine. When he finished eating, he then sat to relax for a few minutes.

"Yo, Huskin?" Seth asked.

"Yeah?" Huskin responded.

"I think I like Lucy," Seth said.

"Ah," Bronco began, "you tryin' to be all cool around the girls so they like you?"

"Of course not," Seth said. "Okay, fine, yes. So I like the girl, and she makes me feel all warm and good. And I screw up on my words when she talks to me. But I like the girl. I'll rip someone in half if they dare try to hurt her."

"You like the girl that much?" Huskin asked.

The X Hounds

"More than that," Seth responded.

"Don't feel embarrassed or anything," Bronco said. "'Cause to be honest, I feel the exact same way about Brittany."

"You're not alone, boys," Huskin said. "If Emily is not in my life till I die, life means nothing to me, and there's no point in living it. So I say we all do something for the girls we like." They stood in a corner waiting for Jaykon to show up. When Jaykon saw them, he looked at them and began running to the bathroom, trying to run away. He jumped out of the window, and the boys chased after him with the strap, duct tape, and flour, but what Jaykon didn't know was that he was running right toward the invisible ship. Running at top speed, Jaykon ended up finding himself running at no speed. So yeah, he ran straight into the invisible ship.

"It's an invisible ship, not an undodgeable ship!" Seth yelled. They ran to him while he was down, and Huskin was striking him with the strap. After ten lashes, he screamed out in pain with his eyes and his mouth wide open. That gave Bronco the opportunity to throw the flour in his eyes so he couldn't see. He screamed out even more, and Bronco threw flour in his mouth so he'd stop screaming. Jaykon then realized that it was over. Seth then wrapped him in duct tape, and they threw him in the pit of the ship, which was where they could leave criminals so they wouldn't mess with the ship. Once they were all on the ship, they headed back to Baron's lair to make the sacrifice for him. Once they arrived at Baron's throne, they presented Jaykon to him.

"Here he is, Baron," Huskin said. Baron turned his chair around to look and had a look of great disbelief in his eyes. He never thought that anyone would ever be able to capture Jaykon.

"Well done," Baron said. "I will admit I kind of underestimated you three. But now I will relieve you of your great evil. Throw him in the portal of banishment." The portal of banishment was an eternal suffering for your wrongdoings. It was exclusively for criminals. There is a suffering of never being able to stop falling, and if you do stop, your death is two hours away. But no matter what, anything can happen when in the portal.

Thick Brick

They threw him into the portal, and after that, Huskin asked, "What was the purpose of this whole thing?"

"Watch," Baron responded. While they heard the screeching of Jaykon, a shiny blue liquid came dripping out of the fountain hose and into three glass cups. Baron walked over to the fountain and grabbed the tray with the three glass cups on it. He then walked over to Huskin, Bronco, and Seth and said, "Drink this."

"Why?" Seth asked.

"Trust me," Baron responded. The three men drank from the glass cups, and they began to feel a tingle inside. Within seconds, they were fully removed from the hairiness and the demonic evil which lies in their hearts. Shortly after, a blue X appeared on the right side of their neck. Brittany, Lucy, and Emily noticed this, and they didn't know what to think.

"What's that blue X on the side of your neck, Huskin?" Emily asked.

"What blue X?" Huskin replied. He then went to the mirror and looked at himself. He saw the blue X and said, "Baron, what is this?" Baron looked at it for a few seconds but still couldn't figure out what it meant.

"I don't know, bro," Baron said. "Even my great mind can't even begin to think what it could possibly mean."

"Huh, whatever," Huskin said to himself quietly. "Hey, what do you say we go out and celebrate?"

"Great idea," Emily said rather fast.

"Well, what are we waiting for?" asked Lucy. "Let's go." From there on, it would be all fun and games until a horrifying and treacherous civilization would rise.

CHAPTER 5

The Birth of Deadly Evil

While our seven friends were off having a celebration, it's sad to say, a celebration is the last thing they needed to do right now. For it would not be long before a leader of evil would rise up and become a great threat to the people of Amure-X. The cause of his uprising would be the outcome of the tragedy of project 1B86-0D.

When the laboratory exploded, the anti-illness X-venom serum was spread throughout the entire universe and interfered with the asteroid field. The venom had a magnetic force mixed into it which caused multiple asteroids to form together as one. Eventually, the venom became so powerful the asteroid formed into something very unexpected. It transformed, for it was no longer an asteroid and it had become its own planet. The planet even formed its own two species. There were only two species, and there were only one in each breed.

There was the ten-eyed wolf spider, and the other was the dagger-toothed viper snake. Soon after the planet formed, the two met. They eyed each other with a look of great hatred, and it wasn't long before they would go after each other. They ran to each other and

Thick Brick

began to attack. The spider sank his fangs into the snake, and the snake sank his dagger teeth into the spider. Both released from each other, as the snake let out a loud hiss of pain, and the spider let out a loud screech of pain.

After they got back to the fight, the spider stood his ground and was ready to attack. At the same time, the snake coiled up into his striking position and struck the spider. He wrapped himself around the spider and swallowed the spider. But that wouldn't be the end of the battle. With the assumption of the spider being dead, the snake began to slither off.

Not long after, the spider would seek and achieve redemption. For the snake would grow sick, and the spider would, inside of the snake, explode. The snake then stopped moving and died. A few minutes later, the remains of the spider and the snake, along with the dust particles, began to spin together in a circular motion. The dust became a small tornado, and within seconds, there would be a green-eyed fiend, which emerged from the dust.

Not only was the planet full of dust and a giant asteroid, but it was also full of nitro crystals, which were crystals of nitrogen. "In order for me to be small and meek no more," the evil leader began, "I must find the nitrogen, and I shall grow stronger." He searched the planet for hours but eventually found all of the nitro crystals. "And there you go," he said, finding all of the crystals. "I have found it."

There were countless amounts of crystals, and in order to embrace the great power which the crystals held, he had to shove them into his hands and up to his shoulder. He knew it would take far too long to get all the power from the crystals. Therefore, he raised his hands into the air and the crystals started to move. They began to shake, and soon after, they arose from the ground and were floating in the air. He then moved his hands closer, and the crystals formed together into two. He then brought them to his hands and shoved them in sharp end first. Mass amounts of pain were felt, but he literally kept pushing through. He shoved one into his left hand and one into his right hand.

Seconds later, he felt his body transforming. He became extremely muscular. He became a six-foot-seven, three-hundred-thir-

The X Hounds

ty-nine-pound, evil beast. He traveled onto the center of the planet and began hexing. "*Maukay, hooranay, moofaugust, reskpastal.*" This hexing statement resulted in an actual planet with all the standard landforms.

Once created, he took a good long look at what he was surrounded by. "You've done good, man," he began. "You've done good." He kept on looking around at his wondrous creation and said, "Yes. This, this is where my kingdom lies. Right here, on the planet X-Moc." He began to picture his throne, and his hands connected with his mind. This meant that if he thought it, it would soon be brought to life. After a few hours, he took one good look at what he created and grew happier with every second he gazed upon his kingdom.

He then reached his arm out horizontally and declared, "*Falnoc, clafon, flacon.*" As he declared such unique words, there flew a falcon, landing on his fist. "Welcome, my number one servant. I shall call you Moctar the Falcon of Great Evil." He then smiled as he looked at his servant, and the falcon's eyes turned to a glowing green. The falcon then let out a short screech, walked up to his master's shoulder, and looked upon his leader's kingdom.

The man of evil then spoke and said, "I need something to keep watch of this kingdom and keep it clean. I need assistance, I need an army, and I need servants. And I shall call them the Spexvipes. *Hookay, foojo, meesoct, beel, ofoo!*" When he declared this, there arose from the dust the violent and treacherous army known as the Spexvipes. They had a reflection in their eyes—a reflection of a dagger.

Their tails were snakes with venomous fangs so they could use their tails to strike at the enemy like a scorpion, and their claws were like spiderwebs, which they could use to (1) climb up the walls, and (2) rip across the back and chest of their adversaries. Once they arose, there was a reciting of words which pleased their head honcho.

"HEE, BY YAW. HEE, BY YAW. HEE, BY YAW. HEE, BY YAW. HEE, BY YAW."

"SILENCE!" yelled their leader. "I AM YOUR LEADER! THE UNFORGIVING AND MERCILESS VEXTO!" They all cheered and jumped around as they were being led by exactly what they wanted, a hateful and

Thick Brick

deceiving fiend. "WE WILL ANNIHILATE ANY ORGANISMS OF SUCH PUNY AND HOPELESSNESS! WE WILL BE TRIUMPHANT! FOREVER!"

Vexto's army then cheered in excitement, for they longed to see that day: the day of a great fall of the good people. "Now," Vexto began as he turned his back toward his army, "I order you to prepare a meal which has a serving for MILLIONS of servants. WE SHALL FEAST FOR DAYS!" Vexto then smiled and began to enjoy his rule until a servant of great arrogance approached him with a challenge.

"Why do you order such aggravating tasks?" said the servant.

When Vexto heard this, he was filled with rage. He then asked, "Who challenges me?" When no one answered, he grew even more intimidated. Therefore, he turned around, facing his army, and yelled, "WHO CHALLENGES ME!"

The Spexvipes then cleared a pathway toward the servant who smarted off, and Vexto began to slowly make his way to the arrogant servant. Vexto and his servant stood eye-to-eye and toe-to-toe, and Vexto said, "You are of such bravery yet great arrogance, my clone. Tell me, why do you challenge such a high order of evil?"

The servant then responded with, "I live here in your kingdom of a permissible society where I am not ordered to be a slave. And yet here we are, pleasing you. And I will not be bludgeoned by such a cocky yet weary and despicable *bockfrand!*" *Bockfrand* was used as a bad name in the vernacular of the Spexvipes.

Vexto smirked at the servant, and said, "Son, what's your name?"

The servant then answered and said, "Stan."

"Well, Stan, now that we have your insignificant opinion," Vexto began, "I now have"—he then stuck out his tongue and split it into three and presented his blue flaming teeth and finished with—"your consequence." Vexto took his three tongues, wrapped them around the servant, sank his teeth into him, and devoured the servant in one swallow. "See, I just ate Stan the arrogant servant!" The Spexvipes then cheered for a few seconds, and Vexto asked, "Anyone else challenges? No? Smart decision. Get to work."

CHAPTER 6

Shevil Finds Love

Soon, X-Moc would not be the only planet of evil. And Vexto, he would not be the only evil ruler.

It occurred only a few hours after the devouring of the arrogant servant. As a second form of evil would arise, the birth of Shevil would emerge. She would be on a planet which formed their own two species as well. Those two species would be the lemon-dipped gorilla and the gold-brushed hog.

One day, there was a lemon-dipped gorilla. He was climbing the trees and jumping from one to another during her usual joy run by the yellow swamp. She decided to hang out down by the swamp and was unaware of what was behind her. There sat the gold-brushed hog, stalking her from the trees. The hog ran up behind the gorilla and headbutted her in the back, resulting in the gorilla being sent into the swamp.

The gorilla began to slowly be infected by the chemicals in the swamp and would die in a few short minutes. The hog turned around and began to walk away. The hog would also die in a few short minutes. The gorilla leaped out of the swamp and wrapped the hog in her

Thick Brick

arms to drag her into the swamp. The gorilla strangled the hog while it squealed in agony, and eventually, the gorilla would take a chunk out of the hog and it would die. And as for the gorilla—tired, beaten, and defeated—it would drift off into a deep sleep, dying from the poison of the swamp.

Nightfall would later set upon the planet. And there, from the swamp, Shevil would emerge, the carcass of the hog and the gorilla would contract, and the poisonous chemicals would only strengthen it. From this, there formed the woman of evil. She opened her eyes and would walk out of the swamp.

"It is here," she began. "It is here that I build my queendom. For I am the queen. The queen, of Shevil. The queen of Dublex" (Doo-blakes). "I shall build my palace here. But first, I must create my army. Rise. Rise from the ground. You lie beneath it, and now you shall march on it. RISE!" She then raised her hands, and soon after, there appeared her army. They stood amongst her, waiting for her to give orders. She then gave orders to deliver her to open land, and they marched to the area. She then gazed upon the glory of the open land and began to imagine her palace in her head. She then closed her eyes, reached her arms out, and started creating her palace.

Once created, she opened her eyes and smiled, as she loved what she had created. She climbed on top of her balcony, and her servants stepped forward to hear her speech. "My fellow servants," she began, "I am your queen, and you are my servants, the X-Vorcs! I AM VORCA!" They all cheered at the declaration of their queen, and they would begin to serve and commit themselves to her. The first thing Vorca did was sit on her throne and drink a bottle of soda.

"My servant," Vorca began, looking to her right, "make my dinner." Vorca then looked to her left and said, "Tell the rest of the servants to bring a new species of animals. I will utilize them as a secondary army, and I will put armor on them."

"As you wish, my queen," said the servant.

"*Ooh*," Vorca said. "I like you. So respectful." The servant told the rest of the servants to find an army, and they went searching. They began searching for an area with a clean water source, and they found Vorca's secondary army. They used mind control to capture the

The X Hounds

animals, and they brought them back to Vorca's palace. They shouted at her balcony to get her attention, and she viewed them from afar. "What have you brought to me to be my secondary army?" she asked. They then presented an abundance of grey hippos. "Hippos? It's perfect!!! Get the armor on them! They're going to be sweet!" She was thrilled at the success of her servants but would then be discouraged at another.

"Vorca!" yelled one servant.

"You got a lot of nerve to address me with such disrespect."

"Look, you are not my boss. I serve no one!" said the servant.

"Perhaps you have grown out of line and need to be set straight."

"I said what I said," responded the servant. "Do something about it." This angered Vorca. And it resulted in her attacking the servant. There was a brawl in the queen's room, and it was pretty interesting.

There were some graphic and rough choices of words being used. In the fight, there was hair pulling, name calling, and arm twisting. Vorca then pulled her servant up, and her servant said, "You ugly gutless *hotch-morf!*" Vorca would become even more unhinged. She slapped her servant in the face and threw her to the ground, stomping on her face repeatedly. The servant didn't stop. "You have no royalty nor dominance! You're nothing but a despicable tyrant!"

Vorca then stopped, and said, "What am I supposed to do, kill you?"

"Exactly," said the servant.

"I'm not going to kill you," Vorca replied, standing her servant up on her feet. "I'll do this." Vorca opened her mouth and sprayed her servant's face with purple mist. The mist was full of poison and acid. Her servant then hit the floor screaming, as her face began to decay. She then dragged her over to the door, put the servant's foot in between the door and the wall where the hinges were, and slammed her foot in the door multiple times. Her servant screamed even more, to the point of crying. Vorca looked at her two servants and said, "I think she might be a little mist off at me because I spit in her face."

"Well, you know what they say," her servant on the right began, "it's better to be mist off than mist on."

Thick Brick

"Well, that's stupid," said the servant on the left.
"It's LOGIC!" yelled the servant on the right.
"I DARE YOU TO YELL AT ME AGAIN!" the servant on the left responded. "WE'LL FIGHT! YOU WANNA GO A FEW ROUNDS?"
"I CAN GO A HUNDRED ROUNDS!" the right servant yelled back.
"PFFT! HAHAHA!" They both began to laugh uncontrollably, and if you got the joke, you might too.
"ENOUGH!" yelled Vorca. The two servants then jumped to their feet quick and tried to keep a straight face but barely could, as they had a huge grin and giggled nonstop. "You two are a bunch of twelve-year-olds, I swear. We all get the joke. Prepare my ship, I'm going for a flight. Oh, and as for acid girl, let her rot. Throw her in the dungeon. She is of no use to me anyway."
Vorca was waiting for her ship to be prepared, as her servants were making sure that everything was working. "Servant," Vorca began, "is my ship prepared?"
"Yes, Queen Vorca," the servant replied.
"Good," Vorca said. "Is my Bluetooth working?"
"Everything is working," said the servant.
"Great," Vorca answered. She then got into her ship and was off to fly. Then she would soon be aggravated. Her ship was flying, and then it wasn't; she ran out of gas.
Her ship hit the ground and was slowly stopping. Once the ship stopped, she then yelled, "I TOLD THEM TO FILL THE GAS TANK!" Off in the distance, not too far, she spotted an eatery called Foxwell Bar & Grille. "When I get back to my palace," Vorca began, "they're going to pay! But for now, I'm starving." She walked to the bar and knocked on the door. When she knocked, a young, tall, and muscular man opened the door.
"Hello, little lady," he said. "What are you doing out here with all this beauty?"
"Well," Vorca said as her cheeks went red, "looks like someone is interested. I mean, you look rather dashing yourself."
"Really?" he asked. "I was honestly just trying to look like you."
"Tell me your name?" Vorca asked.

The X Hounds

"Pike," he replied with pride. "The master of layin' 'em down." As they both smiled at each other, Pike moved to the side and let Vorca into the bar. They got a table and dined in for lunch.

"So," Vorca began, "what do you lay down?"

"Drinks," Pike answered. "Mainly whiskey. Care for some?"

"Yes," Vorca replied. "I'm quite hungry too."

"Allow me," Pike said. He then snapped his fingers, and the doors to the buffet opened. When Vorca looked at the buffet, there were so many options: pizza, chicken, fries, chips, chocolate, breadsticks, garlic bread, garlic knots, and so much more. They decided to get a little bit of everything, kind of like my taste in music, but that's a story for later on down the road. They sat down and ate but grew thirsty. "How 'bout that whiskey?" Pike asked. He then snapped his fingers, and a few bartenders brought two shot glasses and a tall bottle of common 14 Vorcish whiskey. They grew a little bored, so they decided to have a little fun. They had an arm-wrestling contest, they played pool, and they had some shots.

"Tell me," Vorca began. "The two guys over there, who are they?"

Down the hall, there were two men drinking whiskey, playing cards, and smoking cigars. Pike then answered with, "The big one dressed in black is Big Humberto, and the short one next to him is Lil Wyatt. Of course, you can't be at a bar without having a nickname. Big Humberto was given the nickname of Risky Whiskey, for always taking risks and tappin' it off with some whiskey. Lil Wyatt got the nickname of X-to-Flex. The X stands for moonshine, and flex means he can bend the rules."

"Interesting," Vorca said with a whisper. "Lil Wyatt sounds like a rapper name."

"Hahaha," Pike said laughing. "He can rap to a degree. The good thing is, you can actually understand him."

"Hahaha!" Vorca said laughing. "Straight facts!"

"Look, I'm being straight-up here," Pike began. "I've never had this good of a talk with anyone, and I like you." Vorca then smiled and reached for Pike's hand. But everyone stopped what they were

Thick Brick

doing, as they heard the sound of shattering glass. Someone took a bottle and smashed it over the head of Lil Wyatt.

Lil Wyatt then said, "Hey, hey, bro! What was that fo'! If you assault me, you gotta go!"

Big Humberto then grabbed the guy by the throat and said, "You a brave guy, but you're gonna die. Imma hurt'cha so bad you gonna cry!"

"Wait," the guy began, "I c-can ex...pla...in."

"You bout to get it, dawg," Lil Wyatt began. "In yo' head, you got some fog. Death is courtesy of the sharp-toothed log hogs."

"Yeet!" yelled Big Humberto. As he yelled this, he threw the guy out of the window, and the log hogs came and seized him. The hogs were just regular hogs; the logs were used as a leash, which were holding the hogs together so they would stay together. The log hogs trampled the guy.

"So," Pike began, "I say we do this challenge I heard of."

"What's the challenge?" Vorca asked.

"You take moonshine and whiskey, mix it together, and simply drink it," Pike answered.

"Sounds good," Vorca said. After two or three shots, they started feeling it. If one of them said something, they both laughed like hyenas. A few more came around, and they got carried away. They decided it would be a good idea to get on the end of the bar and slide across on their knees to do a high five. The outcome? Well, let's call it a fail. They slid into each other and fell off of the bar. They passed out, but when they woke up, they were fine. Big Humberto and Lil Wyatt even asked if they wanted to play a game of pool and make a bet.

"All right," Pike began, "if Vorca and I win, we get the place. But if you win—"

Lil Wyatt cut him off and said, "We kill you. We never lose a game, remember that."

"You're on, princess," Vorca responded. They all four smiled, and Vorca leaned over to Pike and asked, "Why do they get to kill us?"

The X Hounds

Pike then responded with, "Ever since I was but a pupil in their teachings, they've hated me because I was low-classed for them. But let's play some pool." They played until there were only five balls: the six ball, the one ball, the nine ball, the white ball, and the eight ball. Pike hit the six ball in, and it was Humberto's turn. Humberto hit the one ball in, and after Vorca's turn, Lil Wyatt would have to hit the eight ball in, and they'd win the game.

Vorca's turn came, and she lined up to hit in the nine ball; and she hit it in. Now it was Lil Wyatt's turn. It became do or die for both teams. Lil Wyatt lined up his shot and hit the eight ball in. But he took a risk. He shot a shot he knew he would never win and lost. Yes, he hit the eight ball in, but the white ball would follow behind it. Therefore, he scratched. Pike and Vorca won the game and celebrated. "Wyatt," Pike began, "I told you never hit the top left. You miss every time."

"You're a big eater but a huge freakin' cheater!" Lil Wyatt said with anger.

"Face it, my brutha'," Pike began, "I ain't like no otha'. You just a rich, spoiled, silver-spoon mutha—"

Big Humberto grabbed Pike by the throat, and he couldn't finish. This would allow Lil Wyatt to speak to Pike before his death. "Listen to the GOAT, you stupid little zygote," Lil Wyatt said.

"Freeze!" Vorca yelled. Humberto then dropped Pike, and Pike began gasping for air.

"W-We need to get out of here, V-Vorca."

"The only place you're going," Big Humberto began, "is Death Lane. You're our servants."

"Number one," Vorca began, "I'm not a servant. I have them. And secondly..." She then took the shine and whiskey and poured it in her mouth and mixed it with acid. She then spit it out at Big Humberto and Lil Wyatt, and she spit out fire. They, along with the rest of the bar and people, caught fire and burned. Vorca and Pike high-tailed out of there, and the bar collapsed to the ground. Storm clouds rolled in, and the fire went out. They ran to Vorca's ship and got in. "I forgot the gas!" Vorca yelled.

Thick Brick

"Here," Pike began, "I'll pour this in the tank." He poured a small bottle of blue eternal gas into the tank, and it started to glow. Her ship started up, and they headed off to her palace.

"Do you have any chocolate, Pike?" Vorca asked.

"Yeah," Pike replied.

"I need some," Vorca said. Pike then gave her a chocolate bar and a bottle of whiskey, and she said, "Thank you."

"So," Pike began, "how's the palace?"

"Great," Vorca said. "I have servants, I have statues erected all across my palace, and I have anything I want.

"There's no reason for someone like you not to have everything you want," Pike told her.

"You're sweet," Vorca told him. "It would be nice if I knew how to make that drink."

"I can make it blindfolded, Vorca," Pike answered.

"Good," Vorca told him. They headed back to her palace, and when they arrived, Pike went to the kitchen to make some drinks. When he was coming back from the kitchen, he tripped over his own foot and fell to the ground, spilling the drinks everywhere. When the bottles shattered, there were six letters in each bottle that were scrambled all over the floor. Pike took the letters and unscrambled them, and he found the meaning of it.

"Yes!" Pike yelled. "The legend is true!"

"What legend?" Vorca asked.

"The legend," Pike began, "is known as the Legend of Two Great Evils. It's said that a bottle of a drink will be smashed, and there will be letters which spell the word *invulnerable*. There also forms a map leading one civilization to the other. Then the two evils would be united as one and become invulnerable."

"Pike, there is no second evil. There's only the X-Vorcs," Vorca said.

"No," Pike began, "somewhere, this map leads to the other civilization."

"Oh," Vorca replied.

"Vorca?" Pike asked.

"What?" she responded.

"You know I think you're beautiful, right?" Pike asked.

"I think you're hot, Pike," Vorca said. They both smiled at each other and headed off to find the other civilization.

CHAPTER 7

Consolidating

"So, Pike," Vorca began, "how did all you guys end up on Dublex?"

"We had to retreat," Pike responded. "We were big-time lawbreakers, and we lived our life permissibly. We did whatever we wanted with no-holds-barred, and law enforcement went against that. Technically it was wrong to break their laws, but we took ships and crash-landed on the planet so we could live our lives any way we wanted to. Then Lil Wyatt and Big Humberto came in and became dictators. So I got tired of it and joined you, and look what we did."

Vorca would respond with, "Annihilated a chain of dictators, wreaked havoc, and fell in love."

"Yeah," Pike answered. "All those things. More chocolate?"

"Did you really just ask me if I wanted more food?" Vorca asked Pike. "Cause if you did, then, of course, I do." Pike then handed her some chocolate, and they continued their journey for X-Moc.

"Need any shine or whiskey?" Pike asked.

"Just a shot or two," Vorca responded. "I can't handle a whole glass right now. Buzzed flying is drunk flying."

"True," Pike said. "What should we call our drink?"

"I got it!" Vorca responded. "Whiskey moonlight."

The X Hounds

"Of course," Pike said. "We take the moonshine and Common 14 Vorcish whiskey and mix it together."

"Perfect," Vorca replied. They flew to X-Moc, and when they arrived, they landed their ship a few miles away from Vexto's throne. The Spexvipes heard the ship land and headed in Vorca and Pike's direction to investigate. Not long before Vorca and Pike would begin to walk to the throne did they feel the ground shaking. Then there was a yell coming from a distance. Pike and Vorca would begin to walk to the throne quicker. But they would stop. They saw off in the distance the Spexvipes running toward them with the intent to kill. Vorca told Pike to stay behind her, and she would take care of the Spexvipes. Before the Spexvipes could even get close, there was an enormous shout ordered from behind them.

"Halt!" Vexto would yell. The Spexvipes would become literally frozen at the command of their leader, and Vexto would walk up to confront Pike and Vorca. "Tell me," he began, "one good reason to let you live, and I'll spare you."

Pike would give an answer and say, "We don't fall under the ring when we run down the ramp at a wrestling event." At this moment, Vexto would lose it. He let out a laugh harder than steel, and he sounded like one of those paper towel machines at a restaurant that are so unbelievably loud. He couldn't stop laughing. He couldn't breathe for five seconds. When he stopped laughing, finally, he said, "Okay, you two are cool." He then unfroze his servants, and they pondered as to why he was laughing. Pike would then tell the joke a second time, and the servants would lose it as well. They headed up to Vexto's kingdom and began to construct a peace treaty.

On the way to Vexto's kingdom, he, Vorca, and Pike had some talking to do. "So, dude," Vexto began, "what's your name?"

"Pike, bro," Pike responded.

"Nice meeting ya, Pike," Vexto said. "If you didn't already know, I'm Vexto."

"I know," Pike said.

"So," Vexto began, "who's the woman?"

"Vorca, dude," Vorca responded. "Pike's girlfriend."

"She's a keeper, bro," Vexto said to Pike.

Thick Brick

"Oh, believe me," Pike began, "I know." He then said in a whispering voice, "I plan on her being my future wife."

"Nice," Vexto replied. "We may now consolidate and fight against those puny organisms known as humans."

"Aye," Pike began, "you just watch yourself."

"Sorry, bro," Vexto responded. They arrived at the kingdom, sat down, ordered dinner, and signed a peace treaty in cursive. Yeah, I know, no one knows what that "ancient writing system" is.

> I, Vexto, King of the Spexvipes, Master of the Falcon Moctar, declare peace and partnership to the uprising of this new society. To this society, I pledge myself as part leader of the X-Vorcs and leader of the Spexvipes.
>
> —Vexto

Next up to sign the treaty was Vorca. Therefore, Veto handed the treaty over to her, and she began to write.

> I, Vorca, Queen of the X-Vorcs, hereby pledge myself to the planet of X-Moc, as part leader of the Spexvipes and the right-hand ruler next to Vexto. Punishment may vary but will be brutal. For if there is any misconception, any conflict, or any behavioral negativity, the individuals will settle the tension in the ring.
>
> —Vorca

After Vorca signed the treaty, she would then hand it over to Pike so he could write his part of the treaty and his signature.

> I, Pike, the boyfriend of Vorca, agree to all of these laws. I support Vorca and Vexto on these laws and decisions as we rule together. I

The X Hounds

am requiring from the Spexvipes and X-Vorcs respect, loyalty, and that you do as I ask you to.

—Pike.

"Now that we have the treaty made," Vexto began, "we can celebrate. I say we should build a bar and arcade and call it Pike's Bar and Arcade, and we could have wrestling events every Friday night."
"Brilliant!" Pike said.
"X-Vorcs," Vorca announced, "you know what to do."
"Spexvipes," Vexto began, "do the same."

CHAPTER 8

Shepherds of Heirobell

Shortly after the announcement, the now united servants would build blueprints and prototypes for Pike's bar.

After prototypes were constructed, Pike, Vorca, and Vexto went around observing them. Vexto picked up two prototypes. One prototype was a room in Pike's bar, and the other, he did not know what it was.

"Servant," Vexto said.

"Yes," the servant answered.

"This prototype looks of no similarity to something of a bar style," Vexto answered.

"I'm well aware of that, sir," the servant said. "It's a statue prototype."

"I have no memory of saying, 'Build a statue,' my servant," Vexto replied.

"You are 100 percent meticulous, sir," the servant said.

"Well, I wouldn't be stupid," Vexto answered. "What's your name, servant?"

"Randall, sir," Randall answered.

"Randall," Vexto began, "do you think I'm stupid?"

"No, sir," Randall answered. "This prototype is this idea I had. I am currently under the assumption that it will be most pleasant to you, Vorca, and Pike. It's a statue to resemble your greatness." Vexto took a longer look at it, and he'd smile at the site of his likeness in stone. Randall would then say, "I do ask of you to please set it down. It's not quite finished yet. I still need to put the finishing touches on the stone, and I also must paint it. These statues will be big. Not as big as my appetite but big. I also ask you to wait patiently, for you will smile at the site of your likeness in stone."

"I like this guy," Vexto said. "Continue your work." Randall would continue his hard work, and Vorca, Vexto, and Pike would walk around, looking at the hard work of the servants.

Three-and-a-half days would pass, and Vorca and Vexto would call a gathering at the throne. Everyone would gather at the throne, and Pike was asked to give some news.

"Pike, give them the news," Vorca said.

"Moctar!" Vexto said. In seconds, Moctar would fly onto Vexto's right shoulder and sit there. "Tell the news, Pike."

"Spexvipes and X-Vorcs," Pike began, "I have an announcement, a few actually. First off, I'd like to thank Vorca for taking me under her wing and making me a part of her journey. Secondly, I want to thank Vexto for the peace treaty we've constructed. Glad we could compromise greatly. And finally, I want to thank all of you. The Spexvipes, the X-Vorcs, all of you. Together, we are united as the most fierce and sadistic evil that there is. We're overall unstoppable. The peace treaty we have created declares that both of our planets will merge together as one planet. Vorca and Vexto will give the statement which will cause our planets to merge. We will then officially be one society!" The Spexvipes and the X-Vorcs then began to cheer, as Vorca and Vexto would then declare the statement. In just a few moments, the two planets would merge together.

Vorca and Vexto then closed their eyes and declared the statement, "*Quexoticael, Zecktoximael, Moanderax`e, Shomadamule!*" After they declared this statement, the planets would slowly move together. A good thirty seconds went by, and the planets would just

Thick Brick

about be merged fully together. In that moment, there would be a blinding ultraviolet, indigo, and blue light. Pike then yelled as fast as he could and said, "Do not look at the blinding light, otherwise you will melt like an ice cream in Florida!"

But, of course, there always has to be that one person in each group who makes you like, *Huh?* At least, that was the case for one Spexvipe and an X-Vorc. They would open their eyes and scream loudly, for they melted like an ice cream in Florida. Once the two planets were fully merged, everyone then opened their eyes and viewed the sight of the new planet. "All right, everyone," Pike began, "we will all now meet at my bar and have some fun!" Everyone cheered and headed to Pike's bar for drinks, games, and a special event.

Anyway, they all made their way to Pike's bar, and when they got there, Pike finally saw the name of his new bar: Pike's Premium Palace. As they were walking to the bar, they heard a Spexvipe say, "Wihoo, I can't wait to get me sum o' dat shinin' flame drink!"

An X-Vorc would then answer him with, "Ye, ye, brutha!"

Pike heard the conversation between the two, and he began pondering to himself. "Shining flame drink?" Pike said.

"They're probably referring to the Common 14 Vorcish whiskey," Vexto said.

"Oh yeah," Pike said. "Now it makes sense." They went into Pike's Premium Palace, and when they got in, it was endless fun. Arcade, buffet, everything. They had so much fun when they got in. The clock read 6:19 p.m., and they would go on for hours.

They played pool, bingo, retro arcade games, today's video games—they played everything. Then the clock struck 9:02 p.m., and it was time for the special event. It would be the special event, which took place every Friday night.

They called the event SXW, which meant Spexvipe–X-Vorc Wrestling. It would take place in the back of the bar, and they had a full venue of seventy thousand sold-out seats. The main event match would be set that night. The main event would be a thirty-man battle royal for the Premium Palace Championship, which meant if you were thrown over the top rope, you were eliminated.

The X Hounds

Ridiculous Rico was the man who had his eye on the title the most. He knew good and well that he wasn't like the other wrestlers. To even be somewhat relevant to the planet, he knew he had to get this title. And believe me, he had a strategy. All thirty competitors got into the ring all at once for the battle royal. The names of the twenty-nine men were Ridiculous Rico, Jack, Brandon, John, Paul, George, Brett, Dean, Randall, Danny, Logan, James, Peter, Bob, Finley, Sam, Kyle, AJ, Shawn, Ron, Nick, Rex, Adam, Vance, Dougy, Zode, Kevin, Aaron, and Ed. The final entrant into the battle royal would be a mystery competitor.

All twenty-nine men would get to the ring, but the final entrant was nowhere to be found; so they went on without him. "The following contest is a thirty-man BATTLE ROYAL!!!" the ring announcer yelled. "And it is for the PREMIUM PALACE CHAMPIONSHIP." The bell rang, and it was on. Everyone was throwing punches and hammering away at each other. Everyone had their eyes set on that title. In about five seconds, three men would be eliminated right off the bat. The first three to go were Jack, Brandon, and John. With twenty-six men left in the ring, the three men who were eliminated went to the bar for a few drinks.

For the next five minutes, the remaining twenty-six were brawling it out with punches. Paul and George would be the next two to brawl out. Paul and George were always adversaries since the day they were born. This was their chance to destroy each other big-time. George grabbed Paul by the back of the neck and began smashing his face into the turnbuckle.

After that, George leaned Paul up against the top rope to fulfill his game plan of elimination. George then ran to the other side of the ring, bounced off the ropes, and made his way to Paul. George lifted up his arm and had the intention of slashing across the torso of Paul, but Paul had other plans. Paul ducked and pulled the top rope with him, leaving George to fly out of the ring at full speed. With Paul being the fourth elimination in the match, he grew furious and stormed off to the backstage area.

Meanwhile, Brett and Dean double-teamed against George to eliminate him, kicking and punching to chop him down until he was

Thick Brick

eventually too weak to retaliate. They then lifted him up into the air, attempting to eliminate him, but he managed to pull himself down to the apron.

Randall spotted this scenario and then developed a strategy to eliminate all three. He decided to go under the bottom rope so he wouldn't be eliminated, grab a table, and set it up behind them. Randall then crawled back into the ring and lined up his shot. He stepped backward to the other side of the ring, and as he did this, George lifted both Dean and Brett straight into the air.

George's idea was to flip both men out of the ring and through the table, but those plans would be foiled. Randall ran up to George and kicked him straight in the face. This caused George, Dean, and Brett to all crash through the table, making three eliminations. That night, Randall set a record for most eliminations at one time in SXW.

With twenty-two competitors left in the ring, there was a little bit more room to move around with. Danny and Logan decided to team up momentarily against James and Peter. Danny and Logan started hammering away at James and Peter. They then took them and set them on their shoulders in hopes of throwing them out of the ring. They walked right over to the ropes, and in that moment, James and Peter threw themselves downward and swung their legs forward, gripping onto the ring ropes. When they swung their legs forward, they pulled Danny and Logan over the top rope and onto the floor, marking two more eliminations.

James and Peter stood up on the apron and began swinging at each other. James kicked Peter's gut, wrapped his arm around Peter's neck, and dropped him face-first onto the apron. Peter then rolled off of the apron and became eliminated. But James's time was coming soon. James took a breather, and it would eventually cost him.

Finnley jumped up in front of him and threw his fist into James's face. James grew dazed, holding on by one hand. Finnley then turned around and witnessed Bob running toward him. Therefore, Finnley ducked down and grabbed Bob by the waist and flipped him over his head and the top rope. As Bob went flying over the top rope, he wrapped his arms around James's neck and took James to the floor with him, creating another two eliminations.

The X Hounds

There are seventeen remaining superstars. Sam decided to go and grab a ladder from underneath the ring, and he brought it into the ring. When he got it into the ring, he set it up and planned to climb it. He was going to climb it to jump onto everyone, but Kyle climbed the ladder too and they started swinging. Punch here, punch there—just trying to make the other fall off.

AJ spotted this sight and smiled because he knew what he was about to do. Kyle and Sam both stood at the top of the ladder, trying to hurt each other. Kyle then wrapped his arms around Sam's neck in a headlock position on top of the ladder. AJ then pushed the ladder over with Sam and Kyle on top. Both men went flying out of the ring for two more eliminations, and in midair, the second most-memorable site of that night happened. Kyle flipped the headlock into a cutter through the announce table. The crowd erupted. Cameras were taking pictures all over the arena. All seventy thousand fans were on their feet in excitement.

Only fifteen more superstars in the match, and everyone started to grow tired. AJ would then pick up Randall, set him on his shoulders, and then spin him in the air and over the top rope onto the floor. "No! RANDALL GOT ELIMINATED!" exclaimed Vexto.

"Oh, son of a Spexvipe. I liked him," replied Vorca.

"That sucks," groaned Pike. When AJ turned around, Shawn kicked him in the face so hard he fell backward over the top rope and onto the apron. While standing on the apron, Shawn kicked AJ a second time, knocking him off of the apron and making another elimination.

Ridiculous Rico soon discovered there were only thirteen competitors left. After he realized that, he then remembered he was the strongest person in the entire match. He grabbed everyone one by one and threw them out of the ring. Rico grabbed Shawn by the arms and swung him around a few times, then he tossed him out of the ring. He then picked Ron and Nick both up by their shirts and threw them into the crowd.

The crowd got angry at these two for crashing into them because they spilled their food and drinks. So the crowd all grabbed their drink cans and began beating up Nick and Ron. All you could

Thick Brick

see was drink cans exploding and the crowd assaulting them. Rex and Adam looked on in laughter until Rico and Vance came up behind them and lifted them over the top rope.

Vance then asked, "How 'bout a high five, Ridiculous Rico?"

Rico then turned to him and said, "What kind of dumb *bockfrand* are you?" If you didn't already know, *bockfrand* is not a good name in the Spexvipe dictionary. Rico then kicked Vance and tossed him over the rope to make the twenty-second elimination in the match. With only seven competitors left—including Rico—Douggy and Zode would fight off against Kevin and Aaron, leaving Ed and Rico to fight it out.

"You know," Pike began, "I'd hate to leave right now, but I need more food. I'll be right back." The competitors remained fighting as Pike left, but in a way, Pike still wouldn't miss the action. Ed punched Rico, but it didn't even phase him. Rico punched right back so hard Ed was knocked off the ground and spun in circles. Rico then dumped him over the top rope onto the floor, leaving six competitors.

Dougy, Zode, Kevin, and Aaron were all near the ropes, fighting. Douggy and Zode both dumped Kevin and Aaron out of the ring, eliminating them, and Rico would come from behind and dump both Dougy and Zode out. Rico, along with the crowd, believed that he had won the match. But they all forgot about one person: the mystery entrant.

The lights went out, and there was total darkness. Then you could see red smoke all around the ring, and you could hear thumping. The thumping turned into thunder, and then lightning struck in the corner of the ring. Then a blueish-white light began flickering repeatedly. Then came a hand coming out of the ring.

Shortly after, the mystery entrant came out of the ring, and he was wearing a mask. The mask was blue with long pointy ears, sharp orange teeth, glowing red eyes, and a long black tongue. Rico stared at the figure in fear, then he ran to attack him. The mystery entrant caught him. He grabbed Rico by the face and slammed him to the mat. He then brought lightning from the sky and struck Rico with

The X Hounds

it. He then used mind powers to lift Rico out of the ring and throw him to the stage. The bell rang and the lights went out.

Finally, the match was over, and a champion would be crowned. In the darkness, the mystery entrant removed his mask. When the lights came back on, everyone saw the site of the Premium Palace Championship being held up by Pike! Vorca was in shock as she yelled, "THAT'S MY BOYFRIEND!" Vexto stood motionless, as if he'd seen a ghost. Pike came to ringside to see Vorca and Vexto. When he got to Vorca, they looked at each other for a little then shared a three-second kiss.

After the kiss, they all headed back to Vexto's kingdom for a second uniting. When they got back, they all gathered everyone together and made two announcements. Pike gave the two announcements to the servants as he stood there, front and center, from the stage. "My servants," Pike began, "I have two more announcements for you. We will have you create a power source tower to ensure everyone and everything will become more powerful. We shall draw energy from the source, which gives us more power to use as we take control of all society. But first, we must do something which makes us twice as powerful. Stand together, raise your hands, and Vorca and Vexto will merge our two palaces together!"

The Spexvipes and the X-Vorcs all cheered and followed orders, and the palaces began moving together. In a matter of moments, the two planets created a bright light and became one. The light stuck around for a few more seconds, and it was a sight so bright it would transform such a being that would look upon the light. Vexto then shouted, "Look not upon the light but away from it! It will transform you!"

And then came along that one person who doesn't take anything into consideration then has to experience a negative outcome. One X-Vorc by the name of Sariah stopped to look back at the light behind her, then the negative effect would be true. And as she stood there staring at the light, she transformed. She screamed at the blinding light, as it burned her eyes, and then she transformed into a pillar of salt and faded away.

Thick Brick

Once they merged both Vexto's kingdom and Vorca's palace together, Vorca gave another announcement. "Our fellow servants!" she shouted.

"We have united as one true society!" Vexto finished. "We are the most powerful vessels upon all existence. And we shall now be known as…" Then all three said at once, "The Heirobell!" All the servants would cheer their evil name, as they would be known no more as the Spexvipes and X-Vorcs but as the Heirobellians. Then the Heirobellians began constructing the tower, as Vorca, Vexto, and Pike looked on with a smile. "I say we should make a message warning the rest of humanity," Vexto said.

"We'll show those puny mortals they shall be enslaved," Pike responded.

"What are we waiting for?" Vorca asked. "Let's get started. We will show them all we are not just the Heirobell but also the shepherds of Heirobell."

CHAPTER 9

Old Friend

As the Heirobell grew into their own society, our old friends dealt with their challenges at the same time.

By the time the Heirobell would be established, our friends headed off for their celebration. So where did they go? The arcade: Rexton Bar and Arcade. They soon realized that their blaster cannons were down and broken. It's not like they had to have them, or else they would die; but they always wanted to be prepared for anything.

"Well," Seth began, "what are we going to do with our blaster cannons? We need those because they're part of the ship's entire functioning."

"I know where to go," Huskin said dramatically. "To the place of a man who was once so ignorant but is now unimaginably smart. Not like Baron-level smart, but not too far from it."

"And who exactly would you be talking about?" Lucy asked.

"I've known him since childhood," Huskin answered. "Seth and Bronco have met him too, not quite sure if you know him, though. It's our old friend, Malechi."

"Rafe?" Bronco asked. "You're not serious."

"Actually, I am," Huskin answered. "I know he was stupid back then, but now he's actually got some smarts and his skills are

Thick Brick

train-building. He's built every train in all of Amure-X. Except for one, which failed and crashed, but it wasn't created by Maletech" (Mal-luh-teck). "Everything he ever built was a success, and he's become the modern-day Mansa Musa."

"So how do we find him?" Brittany asked. Huskin would then pull something from the neck of his shirt, and it was a necklace with a silver ring at the end of it.

"I've had this ever since I could start remembering things," he said. "It took me years to find out what it meant till one day I put it on my pinky and it read the words '*Maua mai so'o se mea*,' which means 'find from anywhere.' But when I touched it, it showed me I could search for someone or something and locate it." He then searched Malechi Rafe, and the exact location popped up. "Maletech Industries," Huskin said. He would then keep it on GPS and go to him for help.

After a while, they reached his office and went inside. Once the bell rang at the top of the door, he looked over the top of his newspaper which read, "LOCAL CONDUCTOR PLANS FOR MILITARY-GRADE TRAIN IN CASE OF FUTURISTIC APOCALYPSE," and an eight-ball-sized structure was the transformation of his eyes. He became so excited to the point of falling backward from his chair before words were uttered. He then jumped from the floor and said, "My friends!"

"Hey, man," Huskin said. "I know you want to talk to everyone, but we don't have much time."

"Okay," he responded. "Let's cut to it then. What do you need?"

Huskin would then say to him, "Our blaster cannons are shot. We need some reinstallments desperately. Can you help us out?"

"Say no more," Malechi replied. "I've got millions. Come look." They would follow him down a hallway filled with darkness and spiderwebs.

"Oh yes, because this isn't at all how people in scary movies die, right?" Brittany said.

"I'm not down here to kill you," Malechi replied.

"Oh yeah, very convincing," Brittany replied.

The X Hounds

"Brittany," Bronco began, "if he kills us, then he has to hide the bodies and have all that clutter and, above all, paperwork. Is that really worth it?"

"No," Malachi responded. "Not at all." Then they came upon a door, and Malechi put his thumb to the door and access was granted. When the doors opened, the lights turned on, and they all gazed upon the Hall of Cannons. "Welcome to the Hall of Cannons," Malechi began. "This is where I keep all the supplies for my latest invention."

"Wow," Seth began. "How many of these can we have, Rafe?"

"Take what you want and go," he replied. "The city's been good to me ever since I founded the brand-new Fountains of the Pure in the park. Therefore, in exchange for cash, which I get a nice cut from every week that's about 80K, I got all these blaster cannons. Seriously, take as many as you need. I have plenty for what I'm working on. Which leads me to my latest invention, the Warfield." When Rafe opened the door, there was a two-hundred-yard military-grade train with cannons on every window.

"Yo, dude," Huskin began, "you'll never have to worry about traffic again."

"True," Rafe replied. "But it's not finished. I have a long way to go when being a solo act. So I guess you can head back once you load the cannons because it's kinda boring around here. I'll help you get the cannons on, and when they're finished, you can go. Sorry, I don't seem too friendly. It's just—I'm trying to get over something very damaging. But I really don't want to drag you into it."

"What is it, Rafe?" Huskin asked.

Rafe then sighed and responded with, "Heartbreak. We were going good. I finally had everything I needed. It wasn't enough. I loved her. I provided her with all my love. I hugged her. I told her how much I cared, and she threw it back in my face. She shut me off, so I shut off from the world. I'm sorry."

"You good, man?" Baron asked.

"Oh yeah, I'm over it now. It's just…it kinda had a long-lasting effect. But let's not drown in reality, shall we? Let's be creative and

Thick Brick

keep the dream alive. And let's go put those cannons on." Within an hour, the cannons were ready, and everyone jumped on the ship.

"Thanks, Rafe," Huskin said.

"Thanks for coming," he replied.

"Anytime," Huskin began. "See you around, Rafe." Then they started the ship and headed off to base.

Rafe stood there and sighed and then said to himself, "I'm not okay, but no one must know for it makes me weak." Our gang then proceeded back to base but would suddenly be stopped by a magnetic force detouring us from base.

CHAPTER 10

The Nurbians

As they flew back to base, the ship stopped moving and then started shaking. "Huskin," Baron began, "turn the ship around."

"I can't," Huskin replied aggressively. "We're caught in some magnet pulling us toward something." As they flew closer, they noticed something round. They took a closer look and realized it was a planet. It was black and blue with a red streak in it, and when they were finally pulled into the planet, they landed on a platform and prepared for battle.

When they got out of the ship, there was a massive crowd full of blue people who had a black streak diagonally along their face. Then came a man on a floating platform in a black jacket, black jeans, and black sunglasses and stood in front of Huskin and asked, "Who are you people?"

"We," Huskin began, "are confused."

"Well, I guess I should introduce myself. I'm Damien Ryker, leader of the Nurbians," Damien said.

"Well," Huskin began, "These are my friends, Lucy, Brittany, Emily (who may bite), Bronco, and Baron. And I'm Huskin."

Thick Brick

Damien then looked at the side of his neck and noticed the blue X. When he realized what it was, he then got hyped up and said, "It's true. There's no way. But the tale is true."

Huskin then looked at him and asked, "What tale?" Then Damien looked back at him and responded with, "The tale of the Burning Man. Come with me, I must show you my place, offer food and drinks, and tell you the tale."

"Food, drinks, and luxury? I'm in," Huskin said.

"Great," Damien began. "Let's get going. Come on to my platform, all of you, and enjoy the ride." They began cruising to his castle and saw miles of land, flowers, rivers, grass, bubbles in the air, gardens, and animals—everything was relaxing and peaceful. "Welcome aboard Ryker Airlines," Damien began. "Feel free to check out the scenery and enjoy our premium glass bottle sodas. Sit back, drink, and relax on our way to the castle of Nurbia." The ride was about twenty minutes long, and once they arrived at the castle, they went straight inside.

When they got inside, they saw the table of food that was nearly endless with more choices of food than your grandmother's house on a family Thanksgiving. They all gathered their food and drinks, sat in the chairs around the room, and waited for Damien to sit down. When he sat down, he then began the tale and said, "The tale of the Burning Man says that a trio with a blue X on the side of their necks are destined to save the universe from all evil, but the only way to do it is to find Three Elemental War Swords on the dark side of Amure-X. Then they must return and cause a sacrifice in the middle of the final war, with the third sword upon the man with the blue X. And he shall make a sacrifice for all, but it must be the oldest of all three. Then will be the birth of the Burning Man."

"Wait," Huskin began. "That means…" Huskin then sighed, and said sadly, "I must die." He then grew scared, for he knew he had until the tale must be fulfilled. Scared, he then asked, "Damien, what's the birth of the Burning Man?"

Damien looked at him and said, "I hate to tell you this, but I don't know."

The X Hounds

"Okay, but here's my thing," Huskin began. "There's no ultimate evil or anything like that in the universe, so how are we supposed to do this?" Before anyone could make another breath, the emergency alarm on Damien's giant computer began sounding off. It would blink in red letters: "WARNING: TRIPLE THREAT. INCOMING MESSAGE." Everyone swarmed to the computer. Damien clicked the video message, and it was of unspeakableness. Nothing but a pure, cold-hearted, and sinful one-minute, unskippable ad.

"I'M GONNA NEED THERAPY FROM THIS!" screamed Bronco.

"THERAPY CAN'T REPAIR THIS!" Lucy yelled.

"THIS IS CHILD ABUSE, AND I'M IN MY TWENTIES!" Baron yelled.

"I WOULD RATHER FIGHT MATT IN BOXING!" Huskin yelled.

"THIS SUCKS!" Brittany screamed.

"GET PREMIUM, THEY SAID!!! MAYBE WE SHOULD HAVE!" yelled Emily.

"I'M DOWNLOADING TO CLOUD EVERY TIME FROM NOW ON!" Seth yelled.

"SORRY TO EVERYONE FOR THE STUPIDITY OF SOCIETY!" Damien yelled.

Finally, the torment was over, and the video began. First they saw darkness, then appeared a door after being slowly zoomed in on. Eventually, the door opened, and there stood three hooded figures in their own personalized cloak. The common shares between the cloaks were strictly their black color and their steel spikes. However, the figure on the left's spikes were bright pink with bright-pink flames simmering off the black cloak. The right figure would also share this appearance, only the spikes and flames would be red. And the figure in the middle would be at similarities with the other two cloaks, only the spikes and flames would be blue. The middle figure with blue spikes approached the screen with one step and began to speak.

"There is to come a revelation of Amure-X and your beautiful society. For death is mere mercy for what is to come of you. You will not survive. Ye shall perish, hurt, ache, break, bust, fail, fall, and die trying. Your time limit is one score weeks before the fall of humanity and the higher rise of the Heirobell. We don't spare cause we don't care. But enough jokes. The Heirobell is brutal, deadly, and will stop

Thick Brick

at nothing to win. You want nothing but to protect your world. We want nothing but to destroy it. So much error and failure of a society. But not for much longer. We shall kill the smart, control the weak, and enslave the stupid. Your world is full of lies, hurt, fiends, and laundry soap eaters.

"Every one of you are all of these. Your world will have no protection, no love, no compassion, no mercy. Everyone will have restrictions on where they can go, what they can do, whom they can talk to, and everything you can imagine. We shall take all food, clothes, and destroy all peace. Everyone shall fight each other. They will fight for food, life, water, clothes, and will be put into coliseums to go to war and fight. Victors shall be spared, and losers shall surrender or suffer. Torment, just what you deserve." The hooded figure of the middle would then step back, and the hooded figure on the right with red spikes stepped forward to speak.

"Nurbians," he began, "X-Hounds, 1-800-WE-THE-HEROES, whatever you want to call yourselves. There will be an event to take place where we fight to the death for leadership even though it's meaningless, considering we will destroy you easily. The war will be the end for peace and all that is good. Basically, you're screwed. You will endure unimaginable pain: broken bones, torn muscles, dislocations, and separations. The war shall be known as the Heirobell Sunfall War. Because your sun will fall to the control of the Heirobell. I'm a man of few words. Because I don't conversate, I annihilate." He then stepped back, and the hooded figure on the left stepped forward to give her speech.

"Stupid illiterate mental idiots," she began. "I just want to say this: we will enslave, torture, kill, blah blah blah. Whatever, you will die. You now ask who are we…" She cut herself off and stepped back, while all three would then remove their hoods identifying themselves. The one on the left with pink spikes was Vorca, the right with red spikes was Pike, and the middle with blue spikes was Vexto. All three of them began to march in a circle and speak simultaneously saying, "We are the Heirobell. *Heev! Byah! Heev! Byah! Heev! Byah! Heev! Byah! Heev! Byah!*"

The X Hounds

They began to sing, "Heirobell, de-breath all, we shall conquer and destroy. We kill them all, and break their necks. We will kill and enslave. We will capture all of you and end your life with no warning."

They finished singing, and Vexto stepped forward and said, "Huskin, we already know who everyone is. Remember Jaykon? Laugh! He was a mere decoy. We put a tracker on him to find out everything. The only reason we warn you without just killing you for no reason is simple: too much paperwork. I'm kidding, we just thought it would be funny to watch you try to win. Even evil has its fun, man. But enough laughing. I would tell you to visit Rafe, but… And, uh, the warfield's done for."

Then Vorca picked up saying, "Hear the sound of the Deathbell. Surrender, kneel, fall."

Then both Vorca and Vexto would look at Huskin and Emily and close with, "To the Heirobell. Gong! Hide, we're coming."

CHAPTER 11

Sword Quest

The screen went black and all the Nurbians, including Damien, ran around and into each other screaming in absolute horror.

"We're scr—" Damien couldn't even finish before Bronco slapped him to the point of silence.

"We're fine, dude," Seth said.

"There's no reason to panic," Brittany said.

"Huskin's gonna lead us, right?" Lucy asked.

"Of course," Emily began. "He always does." Huskin showed he was ready to lead, but on the inside, he would be worse than the Nurbians. He never had to lead a war or train an army; he had no idea what to do. So he thought about it and decided that he would do exactly that: the best he could, along with self-training himself physically and mentally, but would first give a speech. Before the speech, he would have to tame the wild Nurbians.

"Stop running around like a bad child in a restaurant!" he yelled loudly. At that moment, everyone froze and stared at Huskin. Then Damien would make an announcement.

"Nurbians!" he began. "I will allow Huskin to step onto the stage and direct you of our twenty-week training instructions." Huskin would then step onto the stage and give his speech.

The X Hounds

"War," he began, "only for the Uncharted Titans. The ones who prepare their shields and advance into battle. We fight the abominations who fight against us. Which brings us to our enemy, the Heirobell. We have the X-Vorcs; their leader Vorca, who's second-in-charge, and her boyfriend Pike, who's third in control; the Spexvipes; their falcon Moctar; and the leader of everything, Vexto. We only have about ten billion in our army. They have twenty-two billion.

"As a side note, we shall use earpieces to communicate. Over the next twenty weeks, we will be training. We will train in combat, shooting, jumping, running, and reaction time. I will be taking a certain ten thousand to help Malechi rebuild the Warfield. I don't know how much the damage is, but ten thousand can fix it when on the same page.

"After the Warfield is finished, Seth, Bronco, and I will journey off to the dark side of Amure-X to find the Three War Swords. These next twenty weeks are going to be gruesome, tough, and above all, deadly. We will become the Heirobell's nightmare as the adrenaline fills through our soul. As the fire burns deep into our blood, and as the gong shatters the glass across their tower, we will yell saying, 'FALLEN IS THE HEIROBELL!' This is the final war! We will destroy, conquer, annihilate, and most of all, show them who we are!

"They will fall to us via death! WE ARE THE X-HOUNDS!" Everyone would stand up to cheer and clap for Huskin as he would lead his people to the final war. Then he would say one last thing, and the training would begin. "The reward for victory, which is part of the tale of the Burning Man: you will be immortal." After his final words, the training began.

Week 1.

The Nurbians would train ten hours a day, five days a week, every week: two hours of combat, two hours of shooting, two hours of jumping, two hours of running, and two hours of reaction time. There would be screaming, crying, and rage filling through everyone. Damien, Seth, Bronco, Lucy, and Brittany would stay behind

Thick Brick

to train as Huskin, Emily, and the ten thousand Nurbians ventured off to help Rafe.

When they arrived at his hideout, it was perfectly fine. Huskin was suspicious and felt something wasn't right. "Emily," he began, "come with me. Everyone else, stay behind until I say otherwise." Huskin and Emily would step into Rafe's home and find that the inside was destroyed. It was burnt, broken, and torn apart. They looked around to see if Rafe was anywhere around, and when he wasn't, they went to his underground facility. They took the elevator to his office, but on the way, Emily turned to Huskin and said, "Huskin."

He turned to look at her and said, "Yeah?" Then they both froze and stared at each other, both looking into each other's eyes seeing the stars shine. Emily pulled Huskin in close, and they kissed. "I've prayed for this moment," Huskin said.

"What," Emily began, "kissing a girl in an elevator?"

"No," Huskin answered. "Kissing you, holding onto you, being with you, holding hands, everything. I was terrified to say anything before because I'm a nice guy, and they never get anything. All my life, girls acted like I didn't exist, but you came in and gave me a chance. I was once asked, 'Why are you single?' I answered with, 'Cause I love and care about someone the right way,' and in today's society, that's somehow wrong. But I want to be romantic and treat the right girl like my little princess and give her gifts and love her and give her everything she wants, but somehow, some people could have anything and everything and a drink to go with it and it's still not enough. But with you, you are anything and everything I need. I can't breathe without you. You're sweet like lollipops and cupcakes. I want to be your comfort zone. I love you."

Emily stared into his eyes and started to cry while saying, "I feel the same way. I want you to be mine forever." They stared at each other with sparkling eyes for a few moments, and the elevator dinged. When the doors opened, Rafe's whole office was wrecked: piles of small fire, lights dangling and sparking, debris everywhere, broken glass, and so much more.

When they found Rafe, he was buried in a pile of all. They rushed over to the pile to remove the debris until they found a bloody-faced Malechi. They only hoped he was not dead, and when they moved the rest of it, he began to cough. They sat him up in the chair and patted his back to help him breathe, and he uttered small fragments.

"Water…Heirobell…Warfield…destroyed," Rafe said.

"We know, Rafe, we know. Just relax," Huskin responded. "Emily, stay here with him. I'll get water." Emily sat there for a minute as he went on to get water. He then gave it to Rafe, and he drank it. Breathing heavily, he then asked, "Should I get a doctor?"

Huskin would respond with, "Don't worry." He then pressed his earpiece and said, "Nurbians, bring the doctors down here."

"Right away, sir," Doctor Lane responded.

"Thank you," Huskin said. "How you feelin', Rafe?"

"Revenge," Rafe responded. "Get me two AKs, a knife, and an RPG."

"Hold on, Rafe, hold on," Emily said.

"We'll get there eventually," Huskin added. "Right now you need medical attention."

"They destroyed everything," Rafe said. "The Warfield is destroyed."

"Rafe," Huskin began, "they sent us a message saying they were going to destroy us and take over the world. They told us what happened here. They told us about the Warfield, and they think you're dead. But don't worry, we'll rebuild it. But we don't have much time."

Then the elevator dinged, and Doctor Lane came in and ran tests, did normal checks, and asked questions. After that, he found him with two injuries. "Well, Rafe," Doctor Lane began, "Looks like you'll be on the sidelines for six to nine weeks. You have a small leg and forearm injury. They are minor but must be treated. We can provide rehab and physical therapy, and you're expected a full recovery."

"Well, Doc," Rafe began, "I thought it was just gas that cost you an arm and a leg."

"Heh, heh. Yeah," he responded. He then exited the room and headed back to the ship to get equipment.

Thick Brick

Huskin and Emily then helped Rafe to the elevator via his rolly chair, and he asked, "What are we doing?"

Emily would respond with, "Don't worry about the Warfield. We'll rebuild it."

"How much time do we have?" Rafe asked.

"Twenty weeks," Emily answered.

"We'll never get it rebuilt in that much time," Rafe said. "You would have to have like ten thousand workers to repair it." Then the elevator dinged as they got to the top. The doors opened, and Rafe saw all the Nurbians. He was in immediate disbelief.

He then turned to Huskin, and Huskin said, "We thought of everything. Now on this day, do we build doubt, or do we build Warfield?"

Rafe looked at Emily, then looked at Huskin, and then turned his attention to the ten thousand Nurbians.

"Nurbians!" he began. "We! Build! A WARFIELD!" All the Nurbians then jumped around and cheered, and they salvaged what was left of the weapons in Rafe's lair. There was nothing left there for him, so he moved to Nurb with everyone; and the ten thousand Nurbians loaded the equipment onto their ships and headed back to begin rebuilding.

Week 2.

We now fall upon week 2, and we now know it was only worse than week 1. Training grew harder and more painful. Everyone felt miserable except for four people: Damien, Seth, Bronco, and Huskin. This would be the week in which the Uncharted Titans would venture off for the Three Elemental War Swords on the dark side of Amure-X.

Everyone else was suffering from the ten-hour training period: two hours of combat, two hours of shooting, two hours of jumping, two hours of running, and two hours of reaction time. After all the training, the 9,999,990,000 Nurbians lay motionless, screaming, crying, hurting, throwing up, and every other type of pain imagin-

The X Hounds

able. They laid there for hours and fell asleep. This would continue for the next four days until week 3.

As the Nurbians suffered in their brutal training, the Uncharted Titans ventured off to the Dark Side of Amure-X for the first sword: the Weather-Breaker. When they approached the whereabouts of the Weather-Breaker, they grew more and more aware of how life-risking it would be. The Dark Side of Amure-X is where anything can be, such as the two Jumpers; the Man of the Birds, Lynxer; the Ice-Demon Hailen and their leader, the Skull of the Shadows, who possessed the power of all three.

Finally, they reached the location of the Weather-Breaker and landed the ship to retrieve it. When they landed, there was an extreme snow-and-lightning storm around them.

And on the hill stood the Weather-Breaker wedged into the top of it. They stepped out of the ship one by one and walked to the bottom of the hill. At the bottom of the hill read a sign which stated, "Beware of the two Jumpers."

Huskin and Bronco sent Seth up the hill first to see if he could possess the power of the Weather-Breaker. "I'll head up the hill," Seth began. "You guys watch out for the jumpers." As he stood on the top, he grabbed the sword with one hand, gripped it tight, grunted, and tried to yank it out of the ground. His attempt failed.

"It's okay, Seth," Bronco said. "Just try it again. Try to really feel the power of the sword." Seth took the advice and went for attempt number two using the same technique, only harder and stronger. He attempted this on his second try but to no avail.

"Come on!" Seth yelled angrily.

"Don't stop," Bronco replied. "Grip the sword, feel the power, close your eyes, and squeeze the handle with the strength of a warrior." Then his voice went extremely deep, saying, "BECOME THE WEATHER-BREAKER."

Seth took Bronco's advice like a predator would a wounded prey. He gripped the handle as hard as he could with both hands; closed his eyes; envisioned the snow, the rain, the tornado, and the lightning striking in a simultaneous matter; grunted with the sound of a

Thick Brick

jet turbine; yanked it from the ground upon the hill; and held it vertically above his head, screaming, "I! Am! The Weather-Breaker!"

There came strikes of lightning, roaring thunder, and a snowfall of excess upon him. Then he started floating in the cold air, forming a new set of clothes on Seth: a long cape of snow from his back waving in the wind, lightning veins in his arms and eyeballs, ice shooting from his mouth, and lightning filling through his entire body. As his metamorphosis completed, a horse of all weather would appear under him, and Seth sat on it, holding the sword high into the air.

Then the air cleared, and they heard laughing for a few seconds. They looked around but couldn't find anything. Then they heard laughing a second time, only worse: it grew louder.

"We're getting out of here," said Bronco. They ran toward the ship, and a figure jumped out at them—it was the two Jumpers. They were two snow monsters chained together by the neck and wrists. Before they could even process it, the two Jumpers attacked Huskin and Bronco. They had the chains wrapped around them, trying to kill them, but Seth wasted no time taking the sword and cutting a lightning strike across their necks to decapitate them. When they fell, Huskin and Bronco broke free, and they ran back to the ship and took off.

Now that they retrieved the Weather-Breaker, it was off to find the second sword: the Flame-Riser. While they ventured off to find the Flame-Riser, they still had to be on the watch for Lynxer, Hailen, and the Skull of the Shadows.

When they reached the Flame-Riser's destination, they landed the ship and went to find it. Around them was a bunch of lava, magma, explosions, and a volcano they had to climb to. So they began making their way to the volcano.

It took about two to three minutes after they hopped on the elevator, and they stood at the top, wondering what was going on. When they stepped on top of the volcano, it was completely solid. No explosions, no fire, nothing. There were, however, three pressure plates in the middle of the volcano. The three of them stepped onto the pressure plates, but nothing happened—for the first five seconds. Then appeared in the sky a giant lava asteroid shooting down toward the top of the volcano. They tried to run to the elevator, but the asteroid had already hit and the top exploded, leading them to fall through.

After falling for a minute, they finally landed in a coliseum full of 120,000 fans. Well, fans of the enemy, of course. The Uncharted Titans looked around and couldn't believe what they were seeing. Then they heard the sound of a cage opening, and a figure with horns, red eyes, and birds flying around him appeared. He then said, "I! Am! Lynxer! Man of the Birds!" Only he was no man: he was a dark giant with lava veins, a steel sword, horns, blue wings on his back, and had control over every bird imaginable. "More challengers?" he asked. "This will be too easy. Lower the cage!"

As he commanded this, a steel structure thirty feet in height would lower down. "Welcome!" Lynxer announced, "to rage in the cage!" Everyone cheered for the match as it began.

Then came an announcer, saying, "The following contest is a rage in the cage match! And it is for the Flame-Riser Sword! Introducing the Man of the Birds, Lynxer!" The bell rang and the match began.

Lynxer then charged at all three of them in an attempt to kill them, but when he dove, they all split apart, causing him to go headfirst into the wall of the cage full speed. He then stood up and charged the men again, swinging his sword to try to kill them. Bronco remembers the Weather-Breaker back on the ship and asks Seth to call to it. Seth then calls to it while Huskin and Bronco kept Lynxer and his birds distracted, and in no time, he grasps the sword in his hands.

Shortly after, Lynxer charged him to get the sword, but Seth hit him with a water and lightning combo to shock him entirely and fill his lungs with water so he can't breathe. He also drops his sword in the process, allowing Bronco to capitalize. Lynxer is now weakened but fights it off. He charges Seth once again, but Bronco came up behind him to stab him with his own sword. It did nothing but break.

Lynxer turned around, staring down Huskin and Bronco; and as Huskin took a closer look, he noticed the crown on Lynxer's head.

Thick Brick

The crown controls the birds. He figures if he can jump over him, grab the crown, and smash it, the birds will die off and Lynxer will be all alone. Lynxer began charging Huskin and Bronco, and Bronco got into position to lift up Huskin to launch him over the Man of the Birds.

At the perfect timing, they do just that. Huskin leaps over a charging Lynxer, grabs his crown off his head, lands, jumps up, and stomps the crown, killing all his birds. Bronco ducked out of the way as Lynxer ran full speed into the wall again. This time, he ran so hard he busted through the cage, taking out an entire fan section.

Then Huskin, Bronco, and Seth broke out of the cage and ran to the dark space Lynxer came out of to get away from him. Then Bronco notices the spikes on the door of his cage and immediately begins strategizing a plan to use them. Lynxer stands up, gives a loud roar, and charges their area. "Okay, boys, stand back. I have a plan," Bronco said.

Lynxer is now charging them faster than he ever has before—beyond full speed, angry—and there's no stopping him. But at the right moment, Lynxer jumps into a flight position, spreading his wings and charging the cage. Bronco grabs the lever which controls the door, waits for Lynxer to get closer, and pulls it right when he gets close enough. The spikes go through Lynxer's neck, cutting his head off and killing him for good via Bronco.

Then he grabbed the head, threw it over his shoulder, lifted the lever raising the door, and all three walked out. In the middle of the coliseum, a sword descended down from the sky and would be called the Flame-Riser. Like Seth's horse of all weather, Bronco would get a bird: the Eagle of Fire. The giant eagle appeared under him, and he raised the sword high in the air as Seth did before him. Then there was a sound through the arena, saying, "Volcano will be exploding in one minute."

"Boys," Huskin began, "we need to get out of here." Bronco got on his eagle, and Seth jumped on his horse and allowed Huskin to jump on too. They rode out of the volcano just before it exploded and flew back to the ship to fly out of there before any more explosions. As they flew out of there, they gave a sigh of relief and headed

The X Hounds

on to find the final sword: the Death Fake. So they ventured off to the location of the sword.

Once they reached it, it was a dark mountain full of heavy rain, snow, and strong winds. They landed on the top of the mountain and met the Ice-Demon Hailen and the Skull of the Shadows. The Skull of the Shadows was obviously a skull, but his body was like a normal human. He also had a ripped black cloak and hood. In order to receive the Death Fake, they would have to defeat these final two. All three stepped out of the ship and were confronted by the two.

"Speak your name," said the skull.

Seth then stepped forward and spoke. "Seth," he said.

Bronco fell behind him, doing the same. "Bronco," he said.

Finally, Huskin did the same as the two before him. "Huskin," he spoke.

"Ah! Huskin," Hailen said. "This is the one Vexto told us about."

"You know Vexto?" Huskin asked.

"Of course," the skull began, "we work for him."

"Enough talking," Huskin began. "Tonight, we fight." They stood in position with swords in hand, but Hailen called upon his Ice Demons who began pacing up the mountain at high speed.

"Try getting the sword now, Huskin." Hailen laughed. Huskin stopped, thought for a minute, and realized something.

"Sword. That's it," he whispered to himself. He would backflip toward Seth and Bronco, snatch the swords, and utilize both simultaneously. Huskin raised the Weather-Breaker into the sky, creating a lightning storm intended to strike the Ice Demons to make them fall off the mountain. Then he took the Flame-Riser and wove it in a circular motion, creating a ring of fire around the mountain, causing them to melt away. "This stays between us," he said to Hailen. Then a snowstorm hits randomly, distracting Hailen and leaving Huskin to capitalize.

He took both swords in his hands, stretched his arms all the way out, and slammed them together, creating a shockwave which floors Hailen. Then he put the swords together and created a tornado of fire, sucking Hailen up with it and melting him. All his demons were destroyed too.

Thick Brick

Huskin then stared down the skull and began charging him. The Skull sat there for a minute, letting him charge; and at the last second, he fades to nothing, causing Huskin to fall off the side and drop the swords. Seth and Bronco were under the impression he was gone and was sneak-attacked by the Skull. He slightly wounded them but possessed an intent to kill them. He stood in front of them, laughing, but not for long.

There was a thunder roll and lightning striking, and rising up with wings of fire was Huskin with the two swords. He wasted no time coming up to the Skull from behind, crossing the two swords, and swinging them on the neck of the Skull. His head fell off, but the body still moved. Huskin took the body and threw it off the cliff, piercing it with a sharp icicle on the side of the mountain.

In this moment, each quest was finished. The Death Fake fell from the sky, hovering over the center of the mountain—all three swords had been achieved. Huskin runs up to it and reaches out for the sword. It fades into nothingness, disappearing before he grabs it. Then appears a small card, reading: "Shadow Artificial Intel."

"It was a fake," Huskin began. "There was never a third sword."

"What are you supposed to do in battle, shoot everybody?" Seth said.

"If that's the case," Huskin began to answer, "give me two ARs and an RPG."

"That's it?" Bronco asked.

"Okay, grenades too," Huskin answered. "No time to waste. We're heading back to train hard." And they did just that. They flew back to Nurb and began training hard—harder than the Nurbians.

CHAPTER 12

The Burning Man

Week 3.

Week 3 comes to pass, and training is the same: ten hours a day, two hours of running, two hours of jumping, two hours of combat, two hours of reaction time, and two hours of shooting.

Some Nurbians used guns, and others used a sword and a shield. There would be running up hills, mountains, and creeks. Jumping would include walls, nine-foot dummies, and long gaps. Combat featured actions of hand-to-hand combat, sword-and-shield fighting, and death kicks. Shooting would include running, awareness, targets, and most of all, accuracy. Reaction time was a series of dodging, reversing, jumping up and down, and most importantly, movement speed. Even Huskin, Seth, Emily, Brittany, Lucy, and Bronco trained with them.

Rafe and the other ten thousand Nurbians began drawing blueprints and ideas for the Warfield, hoping to finalize it by week 5 and begin construction. With everybody still screaming, crying, and raging hardcore, no one threw up or laid motionless after. When the

Thick Brick

week ended, everyone would head back home for sleep and everyday lives.

Week 4.

Now arises week 4. Most things end badly in week 4. Don't believe me? Ask your sports team. The Nurbians began to get used to their training and now know what to expect of it. It was still gruesome, but including all Nurbians, there was an improvement rate of one percent.
Seth and Bronco were finding new ways to master their swords for battle. Huskin is suffering but still going strong. Emily, Brittany, and Lucy are holding on as well but still suffering from the pain. The Warfield's ideas were finalized and construction would begin next week.

Week 5.

As we enter week 5 with more rage and determination, the Nurbians begin to feel a 10% decrease in pain during training. Huskin and the girls reach a 1% decrease in pain while training, and Seth and Bronco are growing more powerful with their swords. The Warfield was being built and reached a .5 percent completion rate. Overall improvement rate: 6.9 percent.

Week 6.

Week 6 reaches a new improvement rate but nothing skyrockets. Seth and Bronco grow two percent in skill with their swords. Training reaches a 3% increase, pain decreases by another 7%, Huskin and the girls' skill reaches a 10% increase, and the Warfield is coming along with a 3.5% completion. OIR (Overall improvement rate): 4.20%. NONE of this is intended to be real math; percentages work differently in other realities. Still can't be as bad as the school grading system, though.

Week 7.

As we follow into week 7, we result in a great rise in improvements all around. Everything has grown 10% in improvement. Seth and Bronco are up to 12% on reaching their full potential, training has gone up 10%, the pain has decreased 10%, Huskin and the girls improved by 10%, and the Warfield has grown 10% in completion. For the 10% improvement rate all around, everyone has received an extra upgrade of 6.19%. Overall improvement rate of week 7: 10.33% + 6.19%.

Week 8.

The dexterity for war for our heroes has now become 27.62%, leaving 72.38% to still be accomplished. Everyone trains and follows the routine and comes out on top with a high improvement rate of 12.38%.

Week 9.

We now reach a remainder of 60% to be accomplished, and everyone buckles down by adding an extra hour to each training practice and grasping an additional growth rate of 1.7% along with the standard growth rate of 13.3%.

Week 10.

We are now down to 45% that is left to be accomplished. As in previous weeks, everyone trains harder, following the motto of "Fallen is the Heirobell." The OIR of week 10 grows to 7.5%.

Week 11.

We're down to 37.5%, but somehow, Huskin has made a high improvement rate of 17%. Bronco and Seth make their improve-

Thick Brick

ments too, with Bronco reaching 14% and Seth reaching 12%. But the Nurbians fall 2.5%, leaving their OIR to -2.5%.

Week 12.

With 40% still needed, Huskin decides to increase the difficulty past the maximum level in his own way by adding another hour of training to each practice. At the end of the week, they reach their improvement rate of 15%, as things would really start picking up for them from here.

Week 13.

Now with only 25% left to go, everyone has been improving immensely. Week 13's OIR has reached 19%.

Week 14.

The doors have opened for week 14, waiting to improve from the remainder 6% left to go. And at last, all they must do now is eat healthy to strengthen themselves even more. Everyone is now ready for the final war as they reach the final improvement rate of 16%. They're not just 100%; they went the extra mile and became 110%.

Week 15.

Week 15 would be the same. Everyone was at their full potential and ready to advance into battle. But they spent valuable time, increased the difficulty, and trained more.

Week 16.

Week 16 would be the same as week 15; they just get stronger and faster.

The X Hounds

Week 17.

Week 17 was a repeat of 16.

Week 18.

Eighteen was like 17.

Week 19.

In Week 19, everyone has become so good they reach an additional 4.13% in body improvement.

Week 20.

By Week 20, everyone had a six pack and huge muscles which would increase 3.16% as training was finished.

Final War.

The war has come. They have ventured off to the battlefield to fight the war to end all wars, and they were ready. As for the Heirobell, they were unstoppable. When they arrived at the battlefield, it was a region of no grass and a sunset view. They marched onto the battlefield, processing the fact that this was the end, with the Heirobell inching closer with every step.

At the end of their marching, both sides stood three hundred yards away from each other. Behind the Heirobell stood a tower 3,016 feet tall, where Vexto, Pike, and Vorca stood viewing the war from atop like cowards. A huge dark tower of steel, glass, and spikes pointing at the top of it. They waited for the arrival of the Nurbians, but all that was visible was a cloud of fog.

What emerged from it stood the sight of a true war hero: black military boots with blades on the sides, a navy blue X on the side of the shoe overlapping the blue blade, a navy blue X on the bottom, navy blue shoelaces, black-and-blue military pants, black steel vest

Thick Brick

armor, navy blue steel arm sleeves, a navy blue cape inside with an outside black, black steel gloves which rose up only to mid fingers, long black hair, and a blue bandana tied around his skull. The man of war was none other than Huskin with his two ARs and his RPG ready to save all people.

Huskin stepped forward ten yards and looked forward in the eye of the enemy. "Vexto!" he began. "Surrender and fall to destiny!" The entire Heirobell army burst into laughter, for they did not believe him.

"You idiot!" Vexto would scream laughingly.

"Wait, wait, wait!" he began. "Did you hear him? Me? Surrender? Destiny? Aah! That's a good one!"

He then grabbed his RPG, aimed for the middle of the Heirobell army, and fired away. The rocket hit, disintegrating five Spexvipes and five X-Vorcs, causing their army to go from laughing to quiet. This angered Vorca and Vexto, even though their army still stood at 21,999,999,990. "How are you going to fight with no army?" Vexto yelled.

Huskin then stepped up and said, "I. am. the army." He then began to slowly walk toward the army with his guns ready and stormed into battle. The Heirobell army began charging, but only a few at a time. Then Huskin began jogging as the army ran even faster. Both got closer and closer, full sprinting now at this point. And as the Heirobell army jumped at Huskin, he leapt from the ground, dove through the army, and jumped through the air blasting his 47s in a cyclonic motion. He then landed on the ground, dropped to his knees, and slid across the ground, shooting the enemy. He then rolled through to jump to his feet, fired away at an enemy, and super-kicked him to finish it off.

Then came another enemy he'd shoot at along with the ones all around him, and he wrapped one arm around the neck of the enemy, jumped up, and dropped him to the ground. Huskin then stood his ground and continued to shoot away at the adversaries and anything else that came his way. The next enemy charged him, and Huskin countered with a 360-degree tornado kick to the face which dropped him down to his hands and knees, allowing Huskin to shoot

The X Hounds

at his head, run up, and stomp it into the ground. He then continued to shoot out in a circular motion, striking anyone in his path. These same actions would go on for a few minutes until finally, they stopped charging.

In the process of battling the enemy, Huskin single handedly defeated ten thousand in the Heirobell army. This only angered Vexto and Vorca even more, as he stood up from a kneeling position and stared them down with a killer instinct.

"You fool!" yelled Vorca.

"How are you going to fight all alone?" Vexto asked. "No army, no family, no one on your side! You're all alone!"

"I'm never alone," Huskin replied. Then, emerging from the smoke, came upon his army. He began to recite the chant of the Nurbians he created in his spare time from training.

"Familia!" he yelled. The Nurbians and the rest of his army would repeat every word he said.

"Familia!" they said.

"Protecta!"

"Protecta!"

"Mi Uso!"

"Mi Uso!"

"Defendae!"

"Defendae!"

"Hermana!"

"Hermana!"

"Shieldentae!"

"Shieldentae!"

"Killambe'!"

"Killambe'!"

"Mi Enemae!"

"Mi Enemae!"

Vexto and the Heirobell still laughed, but Huskin then marched forward, ready to fight.

This allowed Vexto to become angry and give the order to Vorca to attack.

Thick Brick

"FIGHT!" she yelled. The Heirobells started running to the Nurbians.

Huskin pointed forward, and his army began marching in. They cocked their guns, banged their shields with their spears, and aimed for the enemy. Then the Heirobells got closer, and the Nurbians jogged. Finally, after being only a hundred yards apart, Huskin yelled, "WE ARE THE X-HOUNDS!" And everyone would run while screaming. The war was on.

From the start, it was pure chaos: Nurbians shooting Heirobells; Bronco riding his eagle of fire, setting them on fire with the Flame-Riser, and hitting them with tornadoes of fire; Seth riding his horse of the weather, sending shockwaves of lightning through the enemy, impaling them with icicles, and shooting cold air mixed with lightning down their throats to electrocute their organs and take their breath away; and Huskin shooting away with his two ARs, leaving him to be untouchable. It was purely no-holds-barred last man standing.

Huskin was jumping over the enemy, 360-degree shooting in the air as if gravity was irrelevant to his very existence. He followed up with kicks, punches, and everything imaginable. He rolled forward, jumped up, 360-degree shot, and drop-kicked an enemy. Then another enemy ran toward him, and he performed the classic duck-down, jump-up, and flip-the-enemy-over-him maneuver. He then finished him off by running up to him, jumping up, wrapping his legs around the enemy's neck, spinning him, and using his legs to throw him to the ground, but it wasn't over. Huskin then ran to him, jumped up, put his boot on the back of his neck, and stomped his face so hard into the ground the dirt would fly up.

Meanwhile, Seth and Bronco would perform a tag team move by each grabbing an enemy by the neck, holding them there for a minute while wielding their swords to fight off other adversaries with techniques such as stabbing, cutting, slicing, and sending shockwaves of fire and lightning through them. Eventually, they would perform a move where they would spin, creating a tornado of fire and weather, and then proceed to slam the two enemies they held by the neck back-to-back causing major pain.

The X Hounds

Rafe drove recklessly through the Heirobell, while other Nurbians shot the enemy from the blaster cannons on the Warfield. Rafe also did donuts to hit the enemy harder. Emily, Brittany, and Lucy would all three shoot away in the battle while also throwing in punches, kicks to the face, throwing their arms across an enemy's chest, jumping knees to the face, and backfists to the teeth. The rest of the Nurbians proceeded with their guns or spears and shields, screeched their battle cry while ridiculously shaking their head side to side as fast as they can, and quickly flicked their tongues in and out of their mouths.

Pure kicks, punches, slaps, slicing, cutting, stabbing, screaming, anger, and shooting would go on for another twenty minutes until Seth, Bronco, and Huskin would all three stumble across each other. Also at this moment, Damien would call Baron to his throne for an important task. He spoke quietly so that only Baron could hear what he would say. After a few minutes of explaining, Baron took off in a ship, leaving the war behind. We now come back to Huskin, Seth, and Bronco.

"Huskin!" Seth yelled.

Which was then be followed up by a "Bronco!" from Huskin.

Then came a yell of "Seth!" from Bronco. "Look!" he continued. "We can take these guys together if we do it like we're in the ring!"

"Good plan!" yelled Seth.

"Fight!" yelled Huskin. They would fight just like the old days in CXW, plus two swords. For ten minutes, it would be a variety of different moves. They jumped over the enemy, grabbed them by the back of the neck, flipped them, then flipped again, dropping them head first. Then each performed a superkick to an enemy. Then Seth and Bronco performed a double superkick to one enemy into Huskin, allowing Huskin to put him on his shoulders and spin-drop him, face first, on the ground. Then Seth and Bronco performed this maneuver a second time, only without the help of Huskin. Then Huskin and Seth performed a double superkick to an enemy. Then it occurred a second time, but Bronco grabbed the enemy and performed a cutter to him.

Thick Brick

Another double superkick came with Huskin and Bronco. They also did it a second time but made the enemy turn around to get a boot to the teeth by a mid-jump Seth. Then each man lined up the shot and ran into their opponent's abdomen head first while shooting at other enemies.

Many more countless moves were performed, leaving the three men alone to drop a good 190 of the Heirobell army. Emily, Lucy, and Brittany would drop a good 100 but with multiple more still to come. While Heirobell lost a total of 290 soldiers, they still had the advantage of 22,999,989,700. The Nurbians still stood at 10,000,000,000 in their army, but the number was about to change big time for Heirobell.

"Seth!" Huskin yelled. "Give me the Weather-Breaker! Bronco! Give me the Flame-Riser!" Both listened to him but still questioned his actions.

"Huskin!" Bronco yelled. "Toss me the gun!" Huskin took the sword and tossed Bronco the gun. Then Seth tossed Huskin the Weather-Breaker, and Huskin tossed him the other gun.

"What are you doing!" Seth yelled to Huskin.

"I'm performing the swords' full potential!" Huskin responded. "Weather! Fire! All loss rainburn!" When he slammed them together and put the two swords at full potential, he could use both of them against the enemy, and he created a burning flood. He then used the burning flood, which is literally just water with fire on it, against Heirobell and burn-washed an amazing 1,999,999,700 soldiers of the Heirobell, leaving only 19,999,990,000 left against the Nurbians. This became a huge advantage point for the Nurbians. Now each person could take almost two at a time to kill and it would be over. But it was not that simple, crediting the incredible strength of the Heirobell and their doubled size, like a Louisiana Purchase. Vorca, Vexto, and Pike all three saw this and grew enraged.

"What!" Pike yelled.

"How are they beating us!" Vorca screamed.

"I will not stand for this!" Vexto yelled. "Release the Heirobell Hippos!" Bet you forgot about them by now, huh? The Hippo army Vorca made her servants search for when she first came

The X Hounds

to life. Yeah, they have armor now. And also…yep, you guessed it: guns which were attached to the armor. The floodgates had opened, and there ran out 69,420 Heirobell Hippos. Huskin realized his people couldn't fight forever. He looked up at the tower and gave it the Eye of Conquer, and made his decision. He made his way running toward Emily to take her on his quest.

"Emily!" he yelled. "Let's go end this!" He reached out his hand for her, and she took it. Holding onto him, he used the sword to fly over the enemy and land at the bottom of the giant tower. He then stared at the top of the tower with the Eye of Conquer, wielded his sword up, and began to fly to the top of the tower. Everyone was still fighting hard but began to grow tired in their fight.

Huskin and Emily decided that in order to stop the war and defeat the Heirobell, they would have to do it themselves. They knew it was impossible; there was no hope, but they still had to fight. They were halfway up the tower and the moment started to sink in. This was it; the war was half over. Everything was looking good, but then it went south.

A Spexvipe was running and crawling up the tower faster than they were flying and caught up with them. Emily and Huskin both caught it, but it was too late. The Spexvipe jumped to Huskin, reached its arm back, and slashed his claws across Huskin's face, causing him to drop the Weather-Breaker and have a hard, fast, and brutal fall to the ground.

Damien witnessed the fall from his throne and flew over to address the damage. Once he got there, he discovered that Emily, due to Huskin breaking her fall, was perfectly fine; but Huskin was brutally injured. While there were no broken bones, he still endured unimaginable pain. He could not walk or move, and he could barely breathe or sit up. "Huskin!" Damien yelled. "Stay with me. It's not over yet."

"Damien," he began. "They're too powerful."

"No, no, no," Damien responded. "We can do this. You have got to stand up and fight. You're about to do something no one else can do, and that's end the war in victory. The Nurbians can fight, but not forever. You have to protect them. You have to defend your

Thick Brick

friends. You have to defend your family, your lovers. You have to defend your name, your values, everything that is important to you. You have to defend your people."

"I have failed everyone," Huskin began.

"No, you haven't," said Damien.

"Where's Emily?" Huskin asked.

"I'm right here," she responded. "Don't quit now. You're almost at the finish line."

"I don't know if I have it in me," Huskin told her. "I'm…sorry. I have…fallen. I don't want to die, but it hurts so bad. I can't die a monster, though. Everything I've done, all the trouble I caused. I have to end the Heirobell." Then he began heavily breathing, forcing three final words. "Fallen…is…Heirobell." His eyes were shut, and he sat there motionless. Damien held his head down, and Emily took his hand whispering,

"I should've told you I loved you." She then closed with a kiss on the cheek and tears rolling from her face as she witnessed the death of her lover.

"You ain't dyin' on us yet, kid," said a random voice in the earpiece. In this moment, the feeling of Emily's lips went through Huskin's body, giving a rush to his veins, mind, and heart. He heard the voice on the earpiece, looked up, and saw Baron with an ARMY OF THIRTY-THREE FIGHTER JETS!

Huskin jumped up and yelled, "BARON! WHERE DID YOU FIND ALL THESE PEOPLE?"

"We're not the only ones fighting Heirobell. Meet the wrestlers from CXW who were stolen from us!"

"Huskin!" the voice began. "It's Carlos Wayne, aka Germ."

"ARE YOU SERIOUS!" Huskin yelled.

"I know what our past is, but we can make it right by defeating the Heirobell!"

"Don't forget about me, Huskin!" another voice said.

"WRECK TOO?" Huskin replied.

"WHAT'S GOING ON OVER THERE, HUSKIN!" Bronco yelled.

"BRONCO!" Seth yelled. "LOOK AT THE SKY!"

The X Hounds

Bronco looked up to see the fighter jets as Rude came on the earpiece to greet them with, "It's me, Rude. Glad I can assist."

"You got rude too, Baron?" yelled Huskin.

"Plus the stolen CXW Superstars!" Baron responded.

"Get 'em locked in and lead the charge of the skies, Baron!" Huskin yelled with excitement.

"Will do, Huskin!" Baron began. "Everyone! Lock in!" All thirty-three fighter jets would then announce their name and address their attendance.

"Jack 76, standing by."
"Germ 17, standing by."
"Wreck 14, standing by."
"Rude 15, standing by."
"Paul Eagle, standing by."
"Brett Raven, standing by."
"John 3:16, standing by."
"Dean 05, standing by."
"George 2012, standing by."
"Randall 25, standing by."
"Danny 2015, standing by."
"Logan 16, standing by."
"James 12, standing by."
"Rico 19, standing by."
"Brandon 2K17, standing by."
"Peter Lion, standing by."
"Bob 2021, standing by."
"Finley 2022, standing by."
"Sam U.D.F., standing by."
"Kyle U.2.A.T., standing by."
"AJ U.3.D.D., standing by."
"Shawn U.4.A.T.E., standing by."
"Ron T.L.O.U., standing by."
"Nick T.L.O.U.P.2., standing by."
"Rex F.G.L., standing by."
"Adam B.T.R., standing by."
"Vance P.H., standing by."

Thick Brick

"Dougy Z.S., standing by."
"Zode 5, standing by."
"Kevin X360, standing by."
"Aaron 6, standing by."
"Ed left on read, standing by."
Everyone was now ready to fight till the end.

"All right, CXW!" Baron began, "Fight!" Once Baron screamed this, all thirty-three jets moved in and blasted hundreds of Heirobell within the course of ten minutes. While the fighter jets were obliterating Heirobell airborne, something snapped inside Huskin, giving him not only the eye but also the intent and heart of conquer.

"Emily," he began, "we're going." She held onto him as they ventured up the tower a second time to finish this once and for all. This time, Huskin took the sword again, and Emily took the two guns to shoot at the enemy if they tried to attack once more. Sure enough, they got halfway up the tower and the enemy gave chase. Huskin then utilized the Weather-Breaker to blast the enemy down the tower, while Emily utilized the two guns to shoot from the other side. Finally, they reached the glass part of the tower, and Vorca, Vexto, and Pike grew more in anger and jumped from their seats to stimulate their fight-or-flight senses.

"Great job, genius!" Vorca yelled to Vexto.

"Why are you yelling at me?" he responded. "This is your fault!"

"My fault!" Vorca responded. Both Vorca and Vexto argued back and forth, while Pike watched Huskin and Emily outside the windows. While the argument was occurring, Huskin performed an amazing air spin and threw the Weather-Breaker through the glass window of the tower, aiming to hit the enemy. The sword was aiming in the direction of Vorca, but she would not see it coming.

"Move!" Pike screamed as he was running towards her. But it was too late. Vorca fell to the floor after a massive shove from Pike but turned around and witnessed something that would break her in every way. There lay Pike, motionless, with the Weather-Breaker stabbed straight through his chest as blood filled his shirt and mouth.

"Pike!" Vorca screamed in fear. She ran to him to pull the sword out, but it was wedged in. She kept pulling and pulling and pulling, but it wouldn't come out.

"It's no use," he began. "I shoved you because I had to save you. My time's up, but yours is now starting."

"No!" Vorca responded. "Don't go. I need you. I love you."

"It's okay, Vorca," Pike responded. "I love you." He then shut his dying eyes and drifted off to the light, laying in Vorca's crying arms. She then went in for one final kiss but went unsuccessful as his lifeless body turned to a cloud of dust and faded out the window into the sunset. Vorca would lay there motionless in tears. Vexto went to grab the sword to attack Huskin and Emily, but they both took the guns and aimed it at him.

"Evil doesn't pay, Vexto," Huskin said.

"I know," he responded. "But it will in 3...2...1." At this moment, Vexto's falcon, Moctar, swooped in and snatched both guns from Huskin and Emily, putting them in Vexto's hands. Huskin and Emily knew they were, sadly, defenseless. He pointed the guns at them and grabbed the sword and proceeded to throw it out the window. Seth then grabbed it while falling from the tower to fight with it again, while Huskin and Emily still faced their issues. "Don't move," Vexto ordered. "Get in the pod, Emily."

Being forced to by the gun, she stepped into the chamber pod and got locked up. He then pointed the gun at Huskin, saying, "Now time for my next prisoner." Then he turned to a heartbroken Vorca and said, "You."

She turned to him angrily with tears down her face, saying, "How dare you turn against me!" She yelled.

"You've done that yourself," Vexto responded. "Get in the chamber."

"I will not do such a thing," Vorca said.

"I said get in the chamber!" Vexto yelled and then shot Vorca's leg for her refusal. "Forget this!" He then lifted his hand and threw her into a pod as well. "Finally," he began. "Now it's just you and me, Huskin. No guns, no swords. Nothing but steel fist brawling.

Thick Brick

"I'm the CXW World Heavyweight Champion. You're about to suffer," Huskin replied. Then he uttered four words which would anger Vexto. "Fallen is the Heirobell."

Vexto's face went bloodshot and his eyes went glass flames. Then both men stood in position, death-stared each other, and took off running. It was happening: the final one-on-one last-man-standing fallout brawl out was underway. Ring the bell, grab the pizza—this is the main event. Straight from the start was punches to the head, bulls locking horns, and taking each other to the ground. Then Vexto rolled on top of Huskin and pounded him over and over until he grabbed Vexto and monster-gripped his throat, causing him to back off. Huskin would kick him in the nose, causing him to back off with a blood-dripping nose. Both men then stood up and stared at each other again, and Vexto would answer with, "Okay, I want blood now."

"I'm breakin' bones, sweetheart," Huskin answered. The brawl would go on and on for a total of thirty minutes until Huskin went for a punch, and Vexto ducked and countered him with a violent kick to the face, which resulted in a fall to the ground for Huskin. At this point, Huskin had nothing left, and he knows it. But he locked eyes to Vexto's chest and hurled his fist into Vexto's chest in hopes to stop his heart.

He connected violently, and it scared Vexto to the point of freezing. Huskin then countered with a right-hook, left-hook, uppercut triple combo. He almost had Vexto on the ground, where he could end it. He waited for Vexto to stand up straight, aimed the shot, and went for a superkick to the face.

Vexto knew he was losing. So before Huskin could connect with a superkick, Vexto ducked and cut the light inside the tower so Huskin would be only a witness of the dark. Huskin couldn't see anything. He then heard footsteps running around and stood alert for whatever was to come next. Then there was a frightening sound of evil laughter, along with a red glowing and flashing body running around the tower with the lights flickering on and off. This continued as Vexto's plan for about thirty seconds.

The X Hounds

Huskin spun around senselessly trying to defend himself as Vexto also ran along the walls and performed weird motions and noises to disturb Huskin. Finally, the room was pure darkness, and Vexto began laughing in a high pitch, saying, "Fallen is the Huskin. Rah!" In the moment of the scream, the lights came on back to full capacity, and Vexto's eyes were a glowing red, with his tongue swinging from his mouth, giving a violent smile as he stood behind Huskin and did something game-changing.

"Aah!" was the scream from Huskin as Vexto took the Deathfake straight through his chest! Vexto was the reason for it disappearing. It was a decoy on the mountain. Huskin slowly began to fall to one knee, hanging his head down toward the ground. He felt the Deathfake pierce straight through his chest and blood dripping from his armor as he shed a tear at the fact that he knew it was over. Vexto then clapped slowly and took a step in front of him and spoke.

"Here lies the hero known as Huskin," he began. "Everything you've fought and trained for, thrown away. The guts, the glory, the sleepless nights. Mr. Save the World Himself. It all meant nothing. If you are anything in this life, it is inaccurate. You're inaccuracy is impeccable. But there is one thing you're right about. 'Fallen is the Heirobell,' as you may say. You're right. Fallen is the Heirobell, and risen are the new beginnings. The beginnings of enslavement, torment, and to me, comedy. Look around you. Look around!" he said, grabbing Huskin by the hair of his head.

"Your strength cannot save you. Your swords could not bring victory to you. Your armor could not barricade death for you. Look at your people. Look at your friends. They could not save you. They could not defeat me or my people. They could not defeat Vorca or her people. Look at them down there. Falling, suffering, fighting with the belief that Huskin is going to save them. It would be a shame to let them down, wouldn't it? Oh well. Let me tell you though.

"We live our early years as a child dying to be a hero, to be noticed, glorified, acknowledged. And we'd do anything to become one. We spend all day wishing we could be the hero. We'd do all the

Thick Brick

fun stuff heroes do: saving the day, chasing the bad guys, kissing the girl.

"But as we grow older and experience life, we wake up one day and see the real world and discover it for what it really is. And in those moments, we slowly begin to realize that the villains are not the bad guys. They wanted one thing: success. And what happened to them? They were broken down, beat up, made fun of, stomped on, and heartbroken simply because they were different.

"As the struggles grow more and more, we then understand the villains. We wake up to realize there are no heroes in this world. Being a hero is a fantasy. But the one and only villain stronger than me is reality. Remember this: the better you are as a person, the more stepped on you are as a man. Now it's time for you to die and watch your little girlfriend cry. If a fantasy makes a man a superhero, reality makes him a villain."

Huskin would have nothing left and stopped fighting it and went motionless. He then looked at Emily in the pod and said his last words.

"Emily," he began, "I love you. I will see you again." He then closed his eyes accepting that he had died trying and faded slowly down to dust. Emily witnessed the entire thing and immediately hit tears. She cried silently for a few seconds and then let out a screeching cry. Vexto turned to Emily and began laughing evilly.

"Shut up!" he said. "You think he loved you? He couldn't even save you. And you know why he couldn't save you? It's not because of him. He died because of you. Maybe if he hadn't tried to save you, he wouldn't have died. Now you will be mine and I shall use you for my personal pleasures because you're just a dumb, stupid HOTCH-MORF!" This was the moment. The defining moment of the entire story.

As Huskin turned to dust with the Deathfake, Bronco and Seth went down, dropping to their knees dropping the Weather-Breaker and the Flame-Riser. Both were then jumped and dogpiled by the Heirobell army. But when the words of Vexto came out about hotch-morf, the dust in which Huskin was reduced to began a small cyclonic motion.

The X Hounds

Vexto then looked back at it in confusion as the dust began to spin faster. Throughout the clouds outside the tower, lightning began to travel to the tower. Then striking the top of the tower, lightning, wind, earth, fire, and every other element of the swords. This would cause the tower to shake as well as the ground. Then the roof began falling apart—glass breaking, high winds, and a partial earthquake.

In the event of these actions, the dust cyclone then began to form a body. It was a new hero to save the Nurbians along with the rest of humanity. When he fully formed, his hair was long and pitch-black with blue flames blazing from it. His clothes and armor were the same as Huskin's, and his whole front body had lightning reflecting everywhere. His cape had a blue flame blazing from the back. His teeth would glow bright as the lightning traveled through. His entire body was as hard as Vibranium. And his eyes were pure lightning with a blazing blue flame for eye color. Seth and Bronco both jumped up and shot the enemies off of them with a blast of their powers. Seth then yelled for Lucy, tossing her the Weather-Breaker.

"You can't do that," she yelled. "You need the Weather-Breaker!"

Seth's eyes then glowed, leaving him to say, "I AM THE WEATHER-BREAKER!" Then he would demolish every enemy in sight while Lucy used the sword. Then Bronco yelled for Brittany and tossed her the Flame-Riser.

"You can't do that," she yelled. "You need the Flame-Riser!"

Bronco then yelled, saying, "I AM THE FLAME-RISER!" Both Seth and Bronco tore through the enemy as Lucy and Brittany slayed their own enemies. Our newest hero was not actually too new, but Huskin in his destined true form. He looked at Vexto with the Eye of Conquer and got ready as he went in for the kill.

"What are you?" Vexto asked angrily. Huskin then gave a three-second pause before saying his name of destiny.

"I AM THE BURNING MAN," he said. These words struck fear into the heart of Vexto as he attempted to run but was thwarted by the Burning Man who sprang from his ground with a blood resulting Vibranium fist to the face. Knocking him into the air, the Burning Man would then connect with a tooth-shattering knee to the face.

Thick Brick

Then he would connect with a four-punch combo with one blow to the right, one left, one uppercut, and a fist to the nose.

The Burning Man then followed up with a triple-knee combo with a knee to the face, a knee to the chest, and then a knee to the side of the head. His next move was a throw to the ground and front-flipping himself, landing on Vexto's stomach. He then yanked him up to connect with a kick to the face followed by putting Vexto on his shoulders and throwing him into the air, spinning him and letting him land on his face.

With Vexto on his hands and knees, the Burning Man Huskin would then jump to the air with his foot on the back of Vexto's head and stomp his face into the floor, causing it to crack. With shards of the floor stuck in his face, Huskin then grabbed Vexto by the waist from behind and flipped him backward, landing on his back. He then quickly set Vexto on his shoulders in a seated position and slammed him to the floor on his back, hitting his head on the floor. Huskin then rolled Vexto backward onto his knees and drove his knee straight into the left eye of Vexto.

The Burning Man then proceeded to yank Vexto up, kick him in the stomach, hook his arms behind him, and drop him on his head. Huskin then connected with a second four-punch combo, backing Vexto up to the glass window of the tower. His next stretch was bashing his face into the glass and then jumping up, wrapping his arms around Vexto's neck, and connecting with a cutter. He then ran up to Vexto, jumped up, placed his foot on the back of Vexto's head, and stomped it into the floor.

Huskin then followed up with stomping Vexto multiple times in the face. Then Huskin would set Vexto on his shoulders in a powerbomb position and connect with a running powerbomb, slamming him to the floor. Huskin's move set of attacks were working; he knew he almost had Vexto. His next move was grabbing Vexto by the face and shocking his eyes with the power of the Weather-Breaker through the Burning Man. He even shocked him so hard he gripped Vexto's left eye and yanked it straight out of socket.

Vexto, of course, screamed in agony but was still getting pulverized by the Burning Man. The arm was the next target for Huskin, as he formed a hammer of hail and flames, which was solid ice with flames blazing from it, and slammed the hammer of hail down on Vexto's right arm. He then proceeded this same tactic with Vexto's left arm, shattering the bones of both.

After the breaking of the arms, Huskin then targeted both legs and obliterated the bones in them. As if the punishment wasn't enough, Huskin formed his hand into a smaller version of a hammer with his fist and unloaded on Vexto's ribs. He then stood Vexto up with a cyclone to hold him up and proceeded to kick him in the face so hard his teeth shattered. He then followed up with a violent fire slap across the cheek of Vexto.

He continued with another four-punch combo to the left and right cheeks of Vexto and jumped up for the final punch across the face of Vexto. Then Huskin built up for something incredible: he slowly began to run around the entire tower and progressively ran faster and faster and faster. Eventually, a ring of lightning, ice, and flames formed, as he ran so fast. It was so bright you could see it from the battlefield.

After some time, Huskin was charged up and ran into Vexto with a rib-shattering spear to the ground. The Burning Man performed this move a second time, forming a second ring of lightning. Huskin then ran up to Vexto, jumped up, and drove a boot of lightning straight to the face of Vexto, causing him to flip backward and land face first on the floor.

Vexto was in excruciating pain. He began coughing up blood and finally threw up twice. Huskin then dragged him to the front of the power source and lay him there suffering. He then freed Emily from the chamber pod and then came for Vorca. Instead of another all-out brawl, Huskin created handcuffs and chains of fire and lightning which would shock and burn Vorca if she attempted to escape. She was then walked over next to Vexto, and Huskin activated the chains. When activated, the chains shocked and burned Vorca, making her go motionless. She couldn't move, so Emily dragged her next to Vexto.

"Here lies Vexto," said Huskin with an evil smirk.

Thick Brick

"Oh, look at you," Vexto began. "I'm Huskin, and I can't even come up with my own lines."

"The drip of your blood," Huskin began, "is what makes me realize how much I'm going to love your death. The enemy's greatest height is their downfall."

"Clap! Clap! Clap! Enough of the crap!" Vexto said clapping. "I don't want some boring hero speech about how you have won and I have lost. Just get on with your garbage. Put me in jail, lock me away, blah blah blah."

"I'm not locking you up," Huskin responded.

"So you're setting us free to take over?" Vorca asked. "Wow, you really are an idiot." Emily then kicked Vorca in the face, busting a few teeth. "Ow! Great, now I look like the yeehoo banjo pickers."

"Don't talk to my man like that, hotch-morf!" Emily said.

"And by the way," Huskin began, "the yeehoo banjo pickers are some of the nicest people ever. It's also pronounced YIHOO!!!!!"

"Well, now that my ears are bleeding," Vorca responded. "Anyway, what are you doing?"

Huskin gave an evil smirk and said, "Sacrifice." The look of fear processed across the faces of Vorca and Vexto. First came fear, then anger.

"IT'S NEVER ENOUGH!" Vexto screamed. "I GO THROUGH HEARTBREAK, THEN GETTING PULVERIZED TO THE POINT OF INCAPACITATION, AND NOW I HAVE TO DIE?"

"YOU'RE NOT THE ONLY ONE, GENIUS!" Vorca exclaimed. Vexto grasped a wave of burning anger for Vorca, turned to her, and spit poison mist into her face, partially melting it. This resulted in a screeching cry from Vorca. But the scream was so hard, and her mouth wide open, that Vexto spit poison mist into her throat, causing her to stop breathing and begin coughing. She was coughing so hard to the point of gagging and was then kicked in the face by Emily. The pain was so bad she passed out.

"Vexto," Emily began. "What do you mean heartbreak?"

"Before I became ruler of the Heirobell," he began. "Well actually, before the Spexvipes alone, I was a lonely soul drowning in the sea of emptiness, begging for someone to love me. I searched and

The X Hounds

searched and searched, but I found nothing. Then it finally came: love. She was the most beautiful, amazing woman ever. Five foot, nine inches, dirty-blonde hair, blue eyes, light-brown skin, hands like silk, and a heart of snow: so pure. The moment I saw her, I was in love.

"I danced around that entire night on the dance floor making everyone laugh, including her. She came over and started dancing with me, telling how I was rocking the dance floor. 'You're rocking the dance floor. I love a guy who can do all that,' she said.

"My heart dropped. My breathing got heavy as I got lost in her eyes and her smile. The most beautiful sight to ever bestow upon. Then I said something risky, but it worked. 'I never thought I'd be dancing with a beautiful woman like you,' I said. She then smiled and told me that's so sweet, and my heart melted. I knew for the rest of my life I NEEDED her. I wouldn't be able to breathe without her. I couldn't take any more sleepless nights alone, lying awake in pain and suffering.

"Swimming in sadness and loneliness, so I had to get her. She then asked me if I wanted to go out for dinner together, and before she finished, I said YES! She then smiled and laughed, and we got out of there and went out to eat. My entire body was shaking in nervousness and excitement.

"After we ate, we played in the arcade for two hours and won so many tickets. I got the giant bear with a heart on it that said, 'You are my heart.' She asked me if I still liked teddy bears and if that's why I got it. I said no and handed it to her.

"Her face lit up. I said, 'It's for you,' and she hugged me tighter than I've ever been hugged before. Then we made our way to the truck, and before we got in, I turned on a song and we danced. Her head on my chest, arms around me, running my fingers through the back of her head, holding her tight, sniffing her beautiful hair. I was home. It was the best feeling of my life. Finally I told her, 'I'm in love with you.'

"She couldn't believe it. 'Is it true?' she asked.

"'Yes.' I responded. I was terrified. I didn't want to lose her, but she had to know what I truly felt. She then stared into my eyes,

Thick Brick

moved in, and we kissed for the last thirty-one seconds of that beautiful song. Fast-forward, and now we're together. We kissed, we hugged, we went out, we stayed in, and we cuddled. It was the best thing in the world. I told her all these wonderful things about her, and she cried and called me romantic. I even had candle-lit dinners and rose petals. That was a mere preview of everything else.

"Finally, the question of a lifetime came. Down by the water, doves in the shape of a heart, the smooth saxophone playing, the flowers. EVERYTHING was there. I knelt down, and as soon as I did, she hit tears. And so did I. I asked her, 'Will you marry me?' She screamed yes, and we had the most passionate kiss ever. As we ate dessert and watched the city lights and the fireworks go off, we knew we'd finally found the love of a lifetime. I would never be happier.

"Then one night, a gang of hooligans came driving through setting fires to our home. Gasoline, lighters, and everything else. Burned the house down for fun. They laughed and drove away. She and I tried to escape, but the roof caved in. Finally, rain came and put out the flames. I woke up with my leg trapped and her next to me with debris piled on top of her. I tried to wake her up as I stared at her bloody face. She woke up and said, 'I love you,' and we kissed for one final time. When it was over, she died.

"I laid there crying, hurting, and waited till I finally died. My human life was over. My new life came once the planet formed with all the chemicals and the snake and the spider fought each other and formed together.

"Then Vexto was born. I swore that I would avenge her and make all humans suffer the pain I did. My plan failed, and here we are." Vexto shed tears and let out a screaming cry. "Daisy. DAISY!"

Huskin and Emily then began to understand. But they still had to end it all. "Defeat me. End it all. I can't take the pain anymore. I know what I must do." He then turned to a woken Vorca and said angrily, "And you're coming with me." Vorca looked at him with fear. She tried to break free but couldn't. Vexto then called upon Moctar to lift her up and stand her on the edge of the reactor shaft.

Once she stood there, Vexto then got Moctar to lift himself up so he could say his final words. "She should've never been with you

The X Hounds

in the first place!" Vorca yelled. "I'm glad she's de—" She was cut off by Vexto grabbing and squeezing her throat, choking her.

"Hear the sound of the Deathbell," he said. She then faded slowly to black, and Vexto dropped her down the reactor shaft. As she fell, he stared at her till she faded off into the distance like a broke even gambler. Vexto then turned himself around, facing Huskin and Emily, and said, "I'm ready."

Huskin then grabbed onto Vexto and asked him, "Any last words?"

"You said it best," Vexto began.

"Surrender, kneel, and fall," Huskin answered.

Vexto then finished with, "FALLEN IS THE HEIROBELL." Huskin then pushed Vexto down the shaft, with Moctar following him. As both Vorca and Vexto fell down the reactor shaft, the tower began to shake and crumble. Huskin and Emily began to dart out of the tower through the broken glass but were thwarted by a pole swinging down, knocking them off the ground. The sad part is, they were hit so hard they fell into the REACTOR SHAFT!

Huskin and Emily began to panic and scream, but Huskin pulled her close and never let go. "I WON'T LOSE YOU, EMILY!" he yelled. "IF I CAN'T LIVE WITH YOU, THEN I'LL SPEND THESE FINAL MOMENTS WITH YOU!"

"I LOVE YOU!" Emily yelled. She then pulled him in for a tight hug and went in for the kiss. The kiss never happened because they disintegrated too fast. The tower of the Heirobell then began to shake and crumble so hard the ground did the same. The Heirobell army began to weaken, and the Nurbians knew the time had come.

"EVERYONE!" Seth yelled. "YELL AND SHOUT AT THE FALL OF THE TOWER!" Everyone stood in position, shooting away at the tower and banging their spears and shields screaming like a mom in the middle of an I'm-the-only-one-that-does-anything-around-here rage. "AAH!"

They screamed until the tower finally collapsed and crumbled to a ground zero. The Heirobell army dropped motionless. But the Nurbians froze at the sight of the tower and slowly walked to the horrific sight of what they feared. Huskin and Emily were gone. And they felt no victory.

CHAPTER 13

A Hero's Sacrifice

They stood a few yards away from the tower and dropped their heads in sadness.

The trumpet of the fallen began to play, and everyone stood there grieving. After the trumpet finished playing, Seth placed the Weather-Breaker upside down into the dirt and set the CXW World Heavyweight Championship around the handles. Bronco would follow a similar choice by placing the Flame-Riser into the dirt right beside the Weather-Breaker. This would represent their grave and everything Huskin and Emily had done. "I thought I could help them, Harley," Damien said to himself silently. "I wish I could've done a better job. I thought the legend was true."

"Damien," Seth asked, "what do we do now?"

Damien put his head down and said, "I don't know." Everyone began to slowly walk away and head back home. Rain began to fall, but Seth, Bronco, Brittany, and Lucy would all stay there to say their final goodbye.

"Huskin," Lucy began, "I can only say one thing: thank you. You made it to the finish line for us. We can now live in peace because of what you and Emily have done. You slayed the beast and saved us all. Thank you. You always made me laugh, always made me feel like

The X Hounds

we had a chance at anything. The way you dance, the way you act. Everything was funny. And when it was time to get serious, you'd instantly become a leader and knew what all of us had to do. You trained the hardest out of anyone, and now you're a warrior. Thank you.

"Emily, you were always like a sister to me. You were there for my first heartbreak. It's like you were there for everything cause you were. You fought alongside Huskin in this war, and you're a hero too. Thank you, sis." She then stepped away and allowed Brittany to speak.

"Huskin," she began. "From now on, every year on your birthday, I will only eat pizza and drink soda to honor you. You were a great friend and an even better man to Emily. Honestly, I wish you two would have gotten together. That's all she dreamed of, was being with someone. And I really wish it would have been you. Thank you for saving all of us. See you around, old friend."

Brittany would step away and Bronco would speak next.

"I don't even know if I can do this," he said. "Huskin," he began, "we've been friends since our training days in wrestling. You and Seth are about the only friends I ever had. I was always the different kid, didn't really fit in. But then I found wrestling. Growing up poor, I had nothing. I don't even know where I'm from. I had to do illegal stuff just to get money for food. I got fired from every job I ever had because I wasn't good enough. I'm not proud of the illegal stuff, but I had to do what I had to do to survive.

"I spent sleepless nights training for CXW and making something of myself so I would have enough money to survive. And then we became breakout stars. We won titles and money and everything. And I never had to worry about whether or not I was gonna eat again. You two are my brothers. Blood or not, you're my brothers. Family's not blood. It's who's been there since day one. I wish you could have gotten with Emily. You loved her the way no one else loved anyone. You're my brother. Thank you." He stepped back and allowed Seth to speak.

"Dude," he began, "you're a war hero. You saved the world. Traded your life for our peace. You deserved Emily. As good of a man

Thick Brick

you were, and the way you talked about her, you deserved her love. And she deserved yours. She was an amazing woman and would've made your life perfect. I'm gonna miss you, man. The champion of the universe." Everyone then turned around and began to walk away. Tears soaked the path back home. Nothing hurt more than losing their friends.

The rain poured harder, and lightning began to strike. Everyone looked in the eye of the storm and witnessed snow falling from the sky. Then a small rumble in the ground began, and storm clouds spun around in the sky. Lightning and fire would strike down at the wreckage of the tower a few times. Then the ground shook harder with the wind blowing at 100 mph.

The Weather-Breaker and the Flame-Riser were shaking like an evil chihuahua. The next thing that happened, they shot up from the ground and emerged from the tower's grave. A newly immortal Burning Man and the Feminine Flame rose from the ashes wielding their swords, lightning and thunder and fire and wind! All coming from the power within!

The Nurbians charged at the sight of their risen heroes. Huskin's black-and-blue armor and Emily's black-and-pink boots, and their blue and pink flame and lightning capes! Everyone cheered as the Burning Man's dragon formed underneath him and the Feminine Flame's dragon formed under her. Huskin and Emily both held their swords high into the air, shouting, "We are the X-Hounds!"

Cheers, cheers, and more cheers at the sight of our risen heroes. Seth and Bronco formed their horses of weather and fire. Brittany hopped on Bronco's horse, and Lucy jumped on Seth's. Everyone celebrated for a few minutes and then traveled back home. Even though everyone was happy, nothing lasts forever. They got back home, and Damien began to feel sick.

"Yo, Damien, you good?" Huskin asked.

"Yeah," he responded. "I still need to get checked, though." Huskin, Bronco, Seth, Baron, Emily, Brittany, and Lucy all followed him to the hospital and sat in the waiting room for the news. The pain of not knowing was scary, but even worse was what they found out. The doctors came out and told them the news, and it wasn't good. They went into the room to speak with Damien and say their final words. "Huskin," he began, "how you been, my boy?"

"The real question is, how have you been?" Huskin responded. "They told us the news. We're sorry."

"Don't be," Damien said. "This is the plan. Come with me."

"Where?" Seth asked.

"Take my hand," Damien replied. "We're going to a place of peace temporarily." Everyone joined hands in a circle and closed their eyes. Once they opened their eyes, they were on a huge grass cliff. Everyone stood there as Damien stood at a distance away from them, saying, "Welcome to the home of the victors. Where every good ruler who wins wars and protects the people spends eternity. This is where I'll remain with my wife, Harley, and I'd like you to meet her." A cloud of dust descended from the sky and formed the body of his wife, Harley.

"Hello there," she said. "I'm Harley, Damien's wife."

"Nice to meet you," Emily replied.

"Have you told them?" Harley asked Damien.

"Not yet," he responded. "Huskin, there's something we need to tell you, Seth, and Bronco."

"What is it?" Seth asked.

"Your bloodline," Damien said. "I'll cut it short. Huskin, you're mother and father are people you've already met. Your last name is a whole lot bigger than you thought it'd be too. Welcome home, Huskin Ryker. We are Damien and Harley Ryker, your parents." Huskin was blown away and in shock.

"Why didn't you tell me?" Huskin asked.

"Because we wanted you to become a warrior first. My time has come. The sun has set on my time as king. Now it's your time, King Huskin Ryker. Take your kingdom. And you will rule alongside your brothers, blood brothers, Seth and Bronco Ryker. That's your heritage. Take my kingdom, son. Marry Emily. We all love the girl."

"I'll never be as good a king as you," Huskin responded.

"I know," Damien said. "You will be stronger. Close your eyes now." Everyone closed their eyes, and Damien gave his final words. "Take my kingdom. Rule with knowledge and humbleness. Celebrate

Thick Brick

my life but cry at my death not. For I have become immortal in this superior land. Acknowledge the hard times and speak of it in praise, for it has taught you to grow stronger."

As he finished speaking, the seven heroes vanished back to the room and shared a moment with the body of their ruler, friend, and father, tearing up and holding onto each other from the loss. Once they headed back home from the hospital room, they held a ceremony for the life of Damien Ryker. Once everyone was together at the ceremony, Huskin spoke for his father to his people.

"Welcome, everyone," he began. "Today we cry not at the loss of our friend, but we celebrate his kingdom, his honor, and his life. He was a great king, a good friend. And even though I only found out a little bit ago, I'm sure he would've been an amazing father. He asked me to take his place as king, as I am his son, as is Seth and Bronco. Together, we'll rule and live a great life.

"When I first met Damien, something felt wrong, and we felt threatened. But as time went on, we talked and grew together as a society. He taught us how to live, lead, laugh, and love. He was one of the best people I've ever known. Right now, we float down the river, a casket filled with flowers, letters, and thank-yous for what he has done for our kingdom. Today, we celebrate Damien Ryker and his last day alive."

Everyone watched the casket float down the river and look to the sky and see his star shining alongside his wife's, and they began to cheer and celebrate his life. The next step was to crown King Huskin.

CHAPTER 14

A New Kingdom

Everyone would plan the coronation for King Huskin and his queen, Emily, at the Nurbian colosseum.

A crowd of billions showed up for their new kingdom come. Music of a new king and queen would sound through the kingdom as they were honored for their rightful place as king and queen.

Baron stepped up and announced the new king and queen. "ALL RISE FOR THE CORONATION OF YOUR LAWMAKERS SETH RYKER, BRONCO RYKER, BRITTANY, AND LUCY!"

Cheers sounded out throughout the kingdom for the lawmakers as they waved their hands to the crowd. The sound of a ringing bell would be made for the acknowledgement of Huskin and Emily.

"THE FOLLOWING ACKNOWLEDGEMENT IS FOR THE KING AND QUEEN OF THE NURBIAN KINGDOM! INTRODUCING FIRST, ACCOMPANIED BY BRITTANY AND LUCY, THE FEMININE FLAME, QUEEN EMILY!" Baron announced. Cheers traveled throughout the crowds for Emily. "AND HER KING," Baron began, "ACCOMPANIED BY SETH AND BRONCO RYKER. THE CXW WORLD HEAVYWEIGHT CHAMPION, THE BURNING MAN, KING HUSKIN!"

Once again, cheers traveled throughout the kingdom even louder as they raised their fists, and everyone threw up their hats to

Thick Brick

the new rulers of the Nurbian Kingdom. After the ceremony, everyone would feast for hours and hours, including desserts. They had everything from pizza, fries, chicken, burgers, and steak to your average holiday dinner. If you thought it, it was there. The same thing for the desserts.

After hours of eating and celebrating, the night came in, and everyone partied to the music. Dancing, laughing, partying the night away—hours of fun, music and fireworks would pass the time in the kingdom. During the partying, Huskin called upon his friends. "Guys!" he said with excitement.

"What's up, man?" Seth asked.

"Woo! This party's rockin'!" Bronco said.

"Dance and party all night!" Baron yelled.

"Live it up!" said Lucy.

"Live like you'll never die!" yelled Brittany.

"Fireworks and music!" Emily yelled.

"Yo!" Huskin began. "I love y'all!"

"WE LOVE YOU ALL!" everyone said at once.

"I love y'all!" Huskin yelled. "HERE'S TO THE GOOD TIMES WITH MY FOR-LIFERS!" As fireworks shot off, everyone cheered, sang, and danced the night away in celebration of Damien's life, the new kingdom, and winning the war.

REMEMBER THIS: IN LIFE, YOU NEVER KNOW WHAT'S GONNA HAPPEN NEXT, AND THAT'S THE BEST PART. Here lies the story of THE X-HOUNDS.

The end.

ABOUT THE AUTHOR

October 12th, 2005, a child born dead, with no hope but a flight from hospital to hospital. Brought back to life, given a second chance. Six weeks in the hospital before being able to come home.

Finally, he made it home and was loved by so many people. Family, friends, church, and preachers. He grew up with the greatest childhood anyone could ever ask for. The movies, TV, music, and video games. I was a major Disney kid, along with Nickelodeon, for movies and TV shows. Video games mainly consisted of Lego, and music was anywhere from pop to country.

When he was nine years old, he eventually moved from Florida to Tennessee and went homeschool for two years. He went back to school in sixth grade and started writing in seventh.

When he was eleven years old, some of his family moved in with him, and he was introduced to a whole new world. His aunt's boyfriend's brother had a video game, WWE 2K17. He started playing it, and after the first few matches, he was a fan. He eventually bought every game after that, and in 2018, he began watching WWE Raw and Smackdown. Ever since then, he was a major WWE super fan.

February 2020, just before COVID, he was watching Raw, and there was a match on that he wasn't too interested in. A random thought popped into his head, and he thought, *I should write a book. But what would it be about?* Then came the idea of a story which consisted of war, mutants, and pro wrestling. He wrote the first chapter and let his middle school teacher read it, and he said, "Keep going. I want to see what you can write."

Ever since then, *The X-Hounds* was born. He wrote the original storyline in five months, but it took years of editing and getting it to be as perfect as possible (it took three to four years). Before finishing *The X-Hounds*, he began writing on a few other projects. Fast-forward to today, and we now have the greatest work he has ever created. Enjoy!